Jack Vance

The House on Lily Street

Jack Vance

The House on Lily Street

John Holbrook Vance

Spatterlight Press Signature Series, Volume 17

Published by Spatterlight Press

Cover art by Howard Kistler

ISBN 978-1-61947-143-6

Spatterlight Press LLC

Spatterlight
P R E S S
340 S. Lemon Ave #1916
Walnut, CA 91789

www.jackvance.com

Jack Vance

The House on Lily Street

Chapter I

Neil Hubbard

At eight-thirty on the morning of Friday June 3, Neil Hubbard turned his Volkswagen north from Bayview Highlands, and arrived in Oakland a few minutes before nine. At nine o'clock he swung into the lot behind the Alameda County Welfare Department, parked in the space marked *Director*. He alighted, walked around the building to the main entrance, a big-bodied man with short legs, a round complacent face. His features were small, set close together; on top of his polished scalp rested a pad of blond hair. He climbed to the second floor, entered the main office, walked up the center aisle, nodding to those senior social workers who happened to be at their desks.

In the reception area before his private office he stopped by the desk where Miss Coyne, his secretary, sat opening mail. Hubbard bent forward in feigned astonishment. "Is that a new hair-do I see?"

"Oh yes," said Miss Coyne. "I thought I'd try something different for a change. I like to experiment with things."

"Psychologists say that's the sign of an alert mind," declared Hubbard. He stretched his arms widely, inhaled, exhaled. "What a beautiful morning! Sunshine, fresh air, not a sign of smog!"

"Yes, it's lovely out," Miss Coyne agreed. "Too nice to stay indoors."

Hubbard made a waggish suggestion: "Let's take the day off and... go fishing. We're only young once; what do you say?"

Miss Coyne laughed. "Now, Mr. Hubbard, you know we can't do that."

"I suppose you're right," said Hubbard philosophically. "As usual."

The telephone buzzed; Miss Coyne responded. "Office of the Director... Yes, he's in." She looked up at Hubbard. "The Police Department on the line, sir. Detective-Inspector Morrissey."

Hubbard took the telephone. "Hubbard speaking." He listened, frowned. After a moment he reached up a hand, pressed down on his flap of blond hair. "I don't quite understand — just a minute, Inspector..." He went into his office, took up the desk telephone. "What's all this again?"

Detective-Inspector Morrissey repeated himself.

"Why don't you just go out and arrest the man?" demanded Hubbard.

Morrissey explained.

Hubbard, still puzzled, said petulantly, "I can't understand how this man Bigg, whatever his name is —"

Morrissey interrupted.

"Certainly a peculiar situation," mused Hubbard. He made a jocular suggestion: "I suppose you've checked in the telephone book?"

Morrissey's voice became crisp. Hubbard pursed his delicate mouth, turned his eyes up to the ceiling. "Naturally I'm concerned. Very much so. But don't forget I'm an old hand at this game. Nothing surprises me any more."

Morrissey spoke further. Hubbard rubbed his hair up into a wispy top-knot. "I agree a hundred percent. It's a black eye for the department. A black eye by association... What's that name again? Biggs?... Oh! That's different. I didn't understand you... I'll talk to the man who works that area... Fine, Inspector, I'll call you back."

Hubbard hung up and heaved a sigh of annoyance. He looked at his desk-calendar, consulted a chart under the plate-glass surface of the desk. He ran his finger along a line, stopped at a name: Paul Gunther.

Hubbard contracted his eyebrows. He flicked down the key of his intercom. "Send in Paul Gunther."

A minute went by, two minutes. Hubbard sat frowning and pinching his chin. Morrissey's news was disconcerting; the longer he considered it the less he liked it. Good public relations could not be taken lightly; if even a breath of scandal touched the department... He looked in annoyance toward the door. Where the devil was Gunther? He reached for the intercom, but at this moment Paul Gunther came into the office:

a dark-haired young man of twenty-five, about average in height and weight with features unobtrusively regular except for a crooked twist at one side of his mouth. He wore a suit of dark blue gabardine, a white shirt with a black-green satin tie — an ensemble which Hubbard, in a fawn tweed jacket and baggy brown slacks, considered over-elegant.

Hubbard indicated a chair; Paul seated himself, waited in an air of respectful attention. Hubbard rolled his eyes to the ceiling and spoke without looking at Paul.

"You have a Mrs. Alberta Baker on your list?"

"Yes indeed," said Paul. "One of our best customers. Lives out on Tenth Street. Four children by four different fathers, drawing the maximum."

Hubbard dropped his eyes from the ceiling. "And Mr. Baker?"

"In jail, says Mrs. Baker. In Wyoming, or maybe Texas; she's not quite sure."

"Any sign that she's cheating?"

Paul shrugged. "Nothing flagrant. She dresses pretty well. I've seen beer bottles and steak bones. No doubt there's a boy friend in the background."

Hubbard grunted. "Well, that's nothing to us unless he's supporting her. Evidently he's not."

Paul raised his eyebrows. "Oh?"

Hubbard leaned forward decisively. "Here's the situation. I've just had a call from the city police. Mrs. Baker complains that she's being blackmailed. Ever hear of 'Mr. Big'?"

Paul nodded. "A casual reference or two, nothing definite. I gather he's a small-time hoodlum. One among many."

"Well, Mr. Big shows ingenuity. He's worked us into his act. According to Mrs. Baker, he's threatened to send proof to the Welfare Department that she's living with a man. She'll be convicted of fraud, she'll go to jail, her money will stop — unless she pays Mr. Big ten dollars a week."

Paul reflected. "Ten dollars a week. Not much of a bite."

"Suppose he's milking twenty or thirty different people? In addition to whatever other rackets he's got going."

"Mrs. Baker is a rare bird," mused Paul. "She seems to have a clear conscience. I'll congratulate her."

Hubbard made an impatient movement. "All this is beside the point. I want to see the thing cleared up; it's the poorest possible public relations." He hitched himself up in his chair. "Inspector Morrissey feels — and rightly, I believe — that if the police go around interrogating our clients, they'll get nowhere. He's asked for our cooperation; naturally we'll help all we can. Here's what I want you to do. During your calls, make a few tactful inquiries. Nothing pointed, nothing heavy. Have they ever heard of Mr. Big? Have they been approached by him? We just want to get the feel of the thing. Follow me?"

"Close on your heels," said Paul. "We're almost neck and neck. In fact..."

"In fact what?" demanded Hubbard.

Paul made an airy gesture. "Nothing important... I take it we want Mr. Big hauled before the bar of justice."

"He seems to be breaking the law," said Hubbard, insultingly polite. "We approve of legality, as a matter of policy."

Paul rose to his feet. "Maybe I can turn something up. I've got an idea or two."

"Remember," said Hubbard, "we're not boy-detectives. Morrissey merely wants us to make a few general inquiries."

"Inquiries yes. Detection no," said Paul. "Got it." He raised his hand in a friendly salute and departed the office.

"Patronizing such-and-such," muttered Hubbard. He leaned forward, consulted the chart under the glass, then spoke into his intercom. "Ask Thorgeson to step in."

On the afternoon of Tuesday, June 7, Miss Coyne buzzed Hubbard, who sat reading one of the numerous official bulletins received by the office. "Mr. McAteel on line 3."

"McAteel. Who's he?"

"Mr. McAteel of McAteel Realty on San Pablo Avenue."

"Whatever he's selling I don't want it."

"I don't think he's selling anything. He asked for Mr. Gunther — in fact he called yesterday — but Mr. Gunther hasn't been in, and he said he'd talk to you."

Hubbard pursed his lips. "Gunther hasn't been in? Not at all?"

"No sir."

"Has he reported sick, anything like that?"

"I don't know for sure, Mr. Hubbard. I'll check."

"Hmff...Well, put on Mr. McAteel."

A contentious voice, pitched in tones of grievance, issued from the receiver. "Mr. Hubbard?"

"Speaking."

"This is Steve McAteel, McAteel Realty. About your man Gunther, I don't feel I should trouble you, but I've tried to contact him personally and had no luck—"

"What's the trouble?"

"Well, I suppose it's really no concern of yours—"

Hubbard said huffily, "In that case—"

"No, no, I mean only that it's Gunther I want to talk to, that your office isn't involved; at least to the best of my knowledge it isn't."

"If I knew what you're talking about," said Hubbard, "I might be able to give you an intelligent answer."

"Well, it's no great shakes," said McAteel. "Let's just call it a matter of inconvenience to me, a lack of consideration on Gunther's part. He came into our office Sunday morning—"

"Sunday morning?"

"We're open every Sunday. Gunther came in about ten o'clock. He said he was interested in one of our properties, a house on Lily Street. I didn't see him personally, he spoke to my salesman, Jeff Pettigrew. He and Gunther are old friends. Well, Pettigrew offered to show the place, but Gunther said he'd look around by himself and took the keys. That's not the way we usually do things, but, well, the house has been up for years."

"So what's the difficulty?"

McAteel's voice took on a defensive pitch. "Gunther was supposed to return the keys the same day, but here it is Tuesday, and no sign of him. I want to know what's what but I can't get hold of him."

"You've tried his home?"

"I don't know his home address. Pettigrew doesn't either. I thought maybe you could help me."

"Strictly contrary to regulations," said Hubbard, on safe ground at last. "However, I'll call myself and let you know."

"Good enough, Mr. Hubbard. I'll be expecting your call."

Hubbard signaled the PBX operator. "What about Paul Gunther?"

"He hasn't reported in, Mr. Hubbard."

"Get me his home."

"Yes sir. I have the number right here in the index." A moment later she called Hubbard back. "Mrs. Gunther, Paul's mother, on the line."

"Hello? Who is this?" inquired a cultivated contralto voice.

Hubbard introduced himself. "I'd like to speak to Paul, if he's at home."

"But I'm sorry! Paul doesn't live with me now. He changed to his own residence, oh, several months ago."

"Perhaps you can give me his telephone number?"

"He has no telephone, Mr. Hubbard. For some reason he decided to do without one."

"Ah," said Hubbard smoothly. "But you have his address?"

"One moment, it's right here... Somewhere... Yes. 1417 Orange Street, in Oakland."

"1417 Orange Street. Thank you, Mrs. Gunther."

"Perhaps I can help?" Mrs. Gunther asked. "Paul discusses all his affairs with me."

"I'm afraid not, Mrs. Gunther. Thank you very much."

Hubbard hung up, waited a moment. Once more he called the switchboard operator: "Put on Mervin Gray, Investigations..."

"Hello," said a quiet voice. "Gray speaking."

"Hubbard here, Mervin. I want you to take a car, run out to 1417 Orange Street. Got that? You're looking for Paul Gunther. One of our men, social worker in Family Services. If he's not there, try to get a line on where we can find him."

An hour later Gray called back. "Mr. Hubbard? You sure you gave me that number right?"

"Certainly I'm sure! What's the trouble?"

"There's no 1417 Orange Street. A 1413, a 1419, and nothing in between."

Hubbard's mouth sagged. "*Somebody* must know where he lives!"

"What's the problem?" asked Gray.

Hubbard cleared his throat. "It's an involved situation. Come on back to the office — or go home, if you like; it's almost five."

"Righto."

Hubbard tilted back in his chair. After a moment he swung forward, brought a bag of dried figs from his drawer. He selected two, replaced the bag, leaned back, munched thoughtfully. He came to a decision. Reaching for the telephone, he called police headquarters and was connected with Detective-Inspector Morrissey.

"Probably I'm raising a hue and cry over nothing," said Hubbard, "but here are the facts. I instructed one of my men, Paul Gunther, to ask around about this 'Mr. Big'. Gunther hinted that he might be able to get some information — he wouldn't say how or where. That was Friday. Gunther failed to report to the office or call in both yesterday and today."

"Is that usual with Gunther?"

"Gunther is more or less irresponsible, but so far as I know he's kept regular hours."

"It could mean something or nothing. Most likely —"

"That's not quite all." Hubbard told of his conversation with Steve McAteel, and described Mervin Gray's inability to find 1417 Orange Street. "I find it all rather puzzling."

Morrissey made a non-committal sound. "I'll put Lieutenant George Shaw on this case. I wonder if you'd tell him what you've just told me?"

"Certainly."

Lieutenant Shaw came on the line. Hubbard repeated his information. Like Morrissey, Shaw reserved judgment. "Of course we'd rather be safe than sorry. You can't get any information at his home?"

"I don't believe his mother knows anything. Either he intentionally gave her misinformation or she's made a mistake."

"Well, tomorrow morning I'll check around, unless Gunther's back at work."

"In which case I'll let you know." Hubbard hung up, and sat with hands resting purposefully on the edge of the desk. Miss Coyne looked through the door. "Anything else, Mr. Hubbard?"

"That's all, Miss Coyne. Thank you."

"Goodnight, Mr. Hubbard."

"Goodnight."

Hubbard sat listening to the sounds of the emptying outer office.

After a moment he rose to his feet, went to the door. The office was now almost vacant. A few people still worked, the clatter of their typewriters strangely sharp and loud. Hubbard went down the center aisle, paused beside Paul Gunther's desk. The surface was clear except for a pair of letters, tucked into a corner of the blotter.

Hubbard seated himself, looked through the drawers, finding nothing of interest. He pursed his lips despondently. His eyes returned to the letters. He reached out, drew them tentatively to the center of the blotter. The first, inscribed in a feminine handwriting, bore the return address: 888 Flores Way, Piedmont. The second, larger and heavier, was directed to G. Paul Gunther, and displayed the insignia of the Bank of America. Without moving his head, Hubbard looked around the office. No one seemed to be watching him.

Hubbard rose to his feet, returned to his own office, seated himself with a grunt of satisfaction. He laid the letters face down on his desk, brought out a knife. With great patience he lifted the flaps.

The letter from the bank turned out to be a monthly statement. Hubbard had expected as much and laid it aside. The second was more emotional in tone. It read:

March 27

Paul:

It's now two o'clock in the morning; I'm alone and worried about myself. What kind of person am I? What kind of person you are makes no difference. I've read somewhere of an artist unable to paint for watching himself in the mirror and wondering "Who am I?" I feel much the same. Who am I? The question won't mean anything to you, nor the answer. It means a great deal to me.

Probably you feel I've failed you; probably you're right. But remember—I say this to myself, not to you—I never made any commitments. You'll agree that I haven't failed myself. This will seem to you a matter of the most sublime unimportance. Because I'm sure I'll never attain that exalted plane upon which you exist. No doubt you have arrived at this same conclusion. In fact I think we've been trying to put together a jig-saw puzzle with pieces from half a dozen different sets.

I know it's late, and I know that circumstances like this make for dramatic insights — and maybe the deepest truths. But I'm writing in the most dispassionate mood I can make for myself. So far I've written only what I could think, reason, rationalize. I'll let you wonder what I'd have to say if I wrote what I felt.

Sincerely,
Barbara

Strange, thought Hubbard. A provocative letter. Reaching into his drawer, he brought forth three dried figs which he ate while he studied the bank statement. "Hm," said Neil Hubbard. "Very interesting indeed." He replaced the letters in the envelopes, resealed them with care.

He telephoned home. "Eunice, I'll be rather late tonight. At least an hour... No, not the slightest... Certainly by all means — I'll have a nice salad when I get home..."

Briskly now Hubbard departed the office.

Chapter II

Jeff Pettigrew

Ten o'clock on the morning of Wednesday June 8, Detective-Lieutenant George Shaw drove an unmarked city car along San Pablo Avenue, a semi-respectable thoroughfare which, from its origin in downtown Oakland, strikes north through a whole series of bayshore communities.

McAteel Realty was located on that segment of San Pablo Avenue bordering West Oakland, a predominantly black district. Shaw parked his car, walked along the sidewalk: a mild-looking man in the mid-thirties, hard and stocky, with a ruff of dust-colored hair.

He entered the offices of McAteel Realty. A receptionist-secretary looked up from her desk. "Yes sir?"

Shaw introduced himself. "I'd like to speak to Mr. McAteel."

The woman asked cautiously, "Does he expect you?"

"I hardly think so."

The secretary rose to her feet, disappeared down a hall. A moment later she returned, nodded toward Shaw. "This way, please."

McAteel was sun-tanned and dapper in light brown Italian silk. His age was about fifty; he was tall, loose-limbed as a rhesus monkey, bald except for a fringe of gray hair over his ears. He jerked courteously half-upright to greet Shaw, motioned to a chair. "Sit down, Lieutenant. What have I done wrong now? Cigarette?"

"No. Thanks." Shaw charged his pipe from a pouch. "I'm here in reference to Paul Gunther."

"Oh yes," said McAteel. "Gunther. The lad isn't in trouble?"

"No, nothing like that. You haven't seen him recently?"

"Not for several days."

"Apparently he's dropped from sight," said Shaw. "Failed to show up for work Monday, yesterday, this morning. No one knows where he lives, and we're wondering what's happened to him."

"I understand that people disappear every day," said McAteel. "Vanish right off the face of the earth."

"I don't want to give the wrong impression," said Shaw. "He might be home sick in bed, for all I know. But as I say, no one knows where he lives."

McAteel shook his head, marveling at the infinite variations of human conduct. "You've checked the hospitals, naturally?"

Shaw nodded, lit his pipe. "No sign of him. I understand that one of your men is a friend of Gunther's?"

"Yes indeed," said McAteel. "I take it you've heard that business about the Lily Street property?"

"Hubbard told me what he knew."

"I'd better call Pettigrew," said McAteel. He raised himself to his feet. "Just one minute." He left the room.

Shaw listened carefully, and seemed to hear the gentle closing of a door. He waited, puffing at his pipe.

McAteel returned with a tall blond young man, muscular and clean-cut, with only the slightest suggestion of softness in arms, legs and jaw-line. McAteel introduced him: "My assistant, body-guard, chief salesman and bottle-washer, Jeff Pettigrew. Also my nephew. Jeff's got a degree in Business Administration; he's going to do great things for us."

Shaw considered Pettigrew dispassionately. He was handsome in a stern pink sort of way, his eyes round, blue, rather prominent. "Well, Jeff," said Shaw, "I guess Mr. McAteel's explained what I'm here for."

"You're inquiring about Paul Gunther."

Shaw nodded. "Do you know his home address, or telephone number?"

"Sorry, we weren't that well acquainted."

"I see. Can you think of anyone who might know?"

Jeff considered, then frowned and said evenly, "No, I'm afraid not."

"In that case," said Shaw, "I'll have to inquire elsewhere."

Jeff nodded graciously. "Sorry I can't help you."

"About that house on Lily Street, did Gunther mention the reason for his interest?"

Jeff shrugged. "I suppose he'd like to remodel and sell — if he can get it cheap enough."

"He's really serious about it, then?"

"Gunther's a strange sort," said Jeff. "You can't always tell what he's thinking."

"I see." Shaw reflected a moment. "I suppose we'd better go take a look at that house."

Jeff nodded without enthusiasm. He opened a drawer, looked glumly through a box of keys. "I hope I can find a way to get in."

"Don't you have duplicate keys?"

Jeff looked up sharply, fixed Shaw with a quick stare of his hard blue eyes. "They seem to be misplaced." He rummaged a moment or two longer. "These should get us through the back door. It's just a common old lock."

Shaw turned to McAteel. "Thanks for your cooperation."

"Not at all, Lieutenant. Hope we can clear things up. The Case of the Missing Welfare Worker, eh?"

Shaw smiled politely. "Something like that."

In the car Jeff Pettigrew allowed himself to relax. "So Paul's missing."

"Not officially. In fact — well, we just don't know what's happened."

Jeff looked sidewise. "Is somebody's money missing too?"

"No," said Shaw. "Nothing like that at all... Incidentally I understand that he's a friend of yours."

"He's not exactly a friend; I've met him here and there, at parties and so forth."

"What sort of a person is he?"

Pettigrew hesitated. The pressure of words built up; his lips trembled; speech came in a sudden gush. "If you want my frank opinion, Gunther's a phony. He's trying to be something he isn't, pushing in where he isn't wanted. You understand what I mean?"

"No, not completely. You mean, he's a social climber?"

Jeff Pettigrew nodded. "That fits well enough. He wants to live like a millionaire on a social worker's income. He wants to act the big shot, but he won't pick up the tab."

"You don't seem to be one of his admirers."

"Hardly."

"Apparently he thinks well enough of you. He came to you about this house on Lily Street."

Jeff laughed. "We have an exclusive on that house. He can't go anywhere else."

"I see... How long have you known Gunther?"

Jeff considered, shrugged slightly. "Six months, more or less."

Jeff and Paul Gunther had met at a party, their encounter catalyzed by a pretty girl named Barbara Tavistock. The date was February 5, the place an old brown-shingled house in Berkeley, on the fringes of the University. Paul arrived at about ten-thirty with a pint of bourbon, to be made welcome by a skinny young man in blue jeans. "Come in, whoever you are."

Paul introduced himself. "Fergus told me to drop by."

"I'm Ira Slavinsky, I live here too." He slapped Paul between the shoulder blades. "March on in. We're informal around here, slovenly in fact. I can't bother to introduce you. Fire escape to the right, can to the left, kitchen straight ahead."

Paul passed through the hall into a large living room paneled in varnished redwood. The furnishings were standard *avant-garde*: a pair of studio couches spread with denim; a record player and large speaker-enclosure; canvas chairs; bookcases crammed with paperbacks. A replica of the Venus of Willendorf occupied the mantle; the walls displayed a group of astounding and chaotic oil paintings; from the ceiling hung an enormous Japanese paper fish containing a string of Christmas tree lights.

Two dozen people occupied the room. Others wandered back and forth along the hall. Paul went out into the kitchen, where he opened his pint of bourbon, secured ice-cubes from the refrigerator, mixed himself a highball. He bent to hide his bottle behind the refrigerator, but the space was occupied by another and larger bottle. Paul tucked the pint behind a platter in the dish-closet, returned to the living room.

He found a seat on one of the couches, and leaning back, considered his fellow-guests. They seemed rather an ordinary group. Everyone had come to watch, to drink, to be entertained. Everyone hoped for adventure, provided it could be accomplished without danger, inconvenience, expense, hangover or scandal. Small chance of adventure here. Where were the daring and beautiful women, the men of character, the talented musicians? No one was even sufficiently offensive to be amusing.

But the evening was young.

A few people he knew by name: Charles Bickerstaff, a pucker-faced little physicist with an obsessive disapproval of government security measures; a tall dark-haired girl named Nausicaa; a flaxen-blonde Greek girl named Iphigenia; Bill and Mary Jones, who eked out the most meager of livelihoods posing for art classes. Next to Paul sat a handsome black youth in a beige summer suit, whom Paul seemed to recognize from another context. None of the girls were especially attractive, but—the evening was young. Someday, somewhere, the miracle; the certainty of this was latent in the doctrine Paul lived by. Someday, somewhere, a surprised meeting of glances, mutual intuition. Paul knew nothing of her, except that she would be radiant with vitality, slender and young and gay, chaste until now, and now suddenly reckless.

Paul began to chat with the young negro beside him. His name was Ted Therbow; he taught economics at night school, worked days at a service station, saving money to emigrate to France. Paul asked in quizzical amusement. "What on earth will you gain by that?"

"Don't be naïve," said Therbow. He added sardonically, "I like good wine."

Paul laughed; Ted Therbow grinned in return. "I know you from somewhere," said Therbow. "Can't figure where."

"School? Berkeley High? Cal?"

"No. Maybe I've sold you gas."

"Might be. Where's your station?"

"Ninth and Van Buren, down in West Oakland."

"I work in that district," said Paul. "I'm with the Welfare Department."

"That's a good job. I'm trying to get into Urban Renewal. Took the test last Tuesday. Lots of slums to tear down out there."

"You want to put me out of work?"

Ted Therbow showed a flash of white teeth. "Sure I'd like to put you out of work. You're not a medicine, you're a bandage. Clean out the slums, give kids a decent chance to grow up. Then there won't be all those hoodlums and delinquents you hear about."

Paul squinted across the rim of his glass. "Do the slums make the hoodlums, or the hoodlums the slums?"

Ted Therbow started to withdraw into a dark imperturbable blandness. Paul said hastily, "I'm not talking about black people. Any kind of people make slums, when they're poor and uneducated."

Ted Therbow still sat stiffly.

"I've got every kind of people on my list," said Paul. "Okies, Mexicans, Blacks, Sicilians, Hindus, even an Eskimo family. I don't see much to choose between them."

Ted Therbow nodded grudgingly. "Ignorant people everywhere, the smart people taking advantage of them."

"I don't deny that," said Paul. "Loan sharks, real estate people, car salesmen, not to mention the home-grown crooks."

Therbow was losing interest in the discussion. "You get into more of that than I do."

"I'm up to my neck in it. You'd be surprised what I run into."

"I guess so. Everybody tries to fool the Welfare Man."

"I just do my job. Why get hung up?" He drained his glass. "I need a refill."

When he returned Ted Therbow had moved, and the empty seats were occupied. A number of other people had arrived; the living room was crowded, the hall clotted so thick as to impede passage to the kitchen.

A woman in pale green teetering on platform shoes lurched into Paul; he put his arm out to support her. She was warm and pliant; Paul held her a moment longer than necessary. She said, "Excuse me, I'm so sorry."

"Not at all. The pleasure is mine."

She wrinkled her nose and moved away. Paul looked after her. About thirty, fairly good figure, rather vacuous in the face. Nothing sensational. She glanced back, turned to him with an arch pout. Paul nodded polite acknowledgement. He finished off his glass. After a pint she might look good.

A third highball went the way of the second and first. Returning to the living room with his fourth, Paul found three couples dancing to music from the record player. He watched, half of a mind to approach the woman in green. He considered her from the corner of his eye. She sat talking to Ted Therbow, who looked bored. When she smiled, Paul saw that she had very small teeth with naked pink areas of gum in between. He decided to wait a few minutes longer.

The bourbon was taking hold. Faces loomed from the shadows, the features important signs which Paul struggled to interpret. Somewhere the key to personality must exist; what power to the man who discovered it! Paul corrected himself. Advantage, yes; power no. Paul had no taste for power. Destiny, whom he knew to be his only real adversary, held a monopoly on real power. Any other sort was illusory. Paul preferred detachment, enjoying his intricate pleasures quietly and intensely. He considered himself a citadel, serene, secure, moving among the complex ways of the world, knowing as much as he cared to know, with pleasure as close as his own imagination... From the kitchen came a gust of laughter. Paul went down the hall to see what was going on. He found several guests leaning against the sink exchanging improper jokes. Paul listened dispassionately. He considered such exercise the pathetic striving of ineffectual personalities. Charlie Bickerstaff, now holding forth, seemed the very definition of the type.

Paul reached for his bottle, poured another drink. He frowned as he saw the level of the whiskey. Two-thirds of a pint gone? Had he drunk so much? He couldn't be sure. Annoying. With a suspicious glance toward Charlie Bickerstaff, he hid the bottle in a new location, and returned to the living room. There still was no place to sit; he stood in the doorway. His consciousness was heightened; his sense of Now was razor-keen; every instant carried a unique and momentous significance... A pale young man in baggy gray flannel slacks, a dark blue sweater worn over a T-shirt, leaned against the wall beside him. Paul studied this young man, considering his function in a universe dominated by the twin entities of Paul Gunther and Destiny. He looked undernourished, not too tidy; his cheeks were hollow, his eyes glittered, his nose was a beak, his hair an unkempt brown thatch. An ascetic? An artist? A poet?

Paul spoke:

> *Into this Universe and why not knowing,*
> *Now whence, like Water willy-nilly flowing:*
> *And out of it, as Wind along the Waste,*
> *I know not whither, willy-nilly blowing.*

The thin-faced young man turned him a wary glance. "Original?"

"Certainly," said Paul, "Here's another:

> *What, without asking, hither hurried whence?*
> *And, without asking, whither hurried hence!*
> *Another and another Cup to drown*
> *The Memory of this Impertinence!*

"That's very lovely," said the thin-faced young man, "but can you make a living at it?"

"No," said Paul, "there's no money in poetry, and money isn't worth going after unless it's easy money. Do you know an easy way to get rich quick?"

"Buy low and sell high; that's the way it's usually done."

Howard Fergus, the co-host, approached. He spoke to the thin-faced young man. "What are you doing here? I thought you worked nights."

"The moon's in the way of my star. Where's Alex?"

"Try the kitchen."

Paul looked after the thin retreating figure. All in all, an uncomfortable man. Unsatisfactory, disconcerting. He turned to Fergus. "Who's that chap?"

"Jim Connor. An astronomer."

"Oh... He's watching a star?"

"One of the exploding type. Now fifty million times brighter than the sun, or thereabouts."

Fergus moved on; Paul remained leaning in the doorway. He

shrugged, put Connor out of his mind. He raised his highball. Marvellous stuff, whiskey. The elixir of dreams. Incorrect. Not dreams. Whiskey sharpened the senses, slowed time. "Excuse me," said Fergus. He pushed into the living room carrying a pot of smoking incense... Senses, thought Paul. Sense and sensation... He closed his eyes, sipped his highball. The flavor of oak and mellow grain. The wetness of water, flowing over his tongue. Sensation: the thud of dancing feet, the reel of his faintly dizzy head. Sound: babble, murmur, a caw of laughter from the kitchen. Close at hand two audible conversations. By some marvellous faculty he could tune from one to the other. But he could not hear both together. Odors: he inhaled. The waft of incense: tobacco smoke; wine; beer. The scent of life, of human breath... A pang of claustrophobic revulsion: "I'm cooped up, jammed in with a herd of humans..." He reassured himself. "I'm human too..."

He walked down the hall into the kitchen, reached for his bottle. His hand met emptiness. The bottle was gone. He looked down, saw it empty on the sink. Paul sighed. He peered behind the refrigerator. A fifth of Old Life Insurance, two-thirds full. Paul poured himself a generous two fingers. Across the kitchen Jim Connor sat eating a piece of yellow cheese. Paul frowned. An issue dangled between them, a matter not yet fully resolved. It was as if Connor had won the first round of a very subtle encounter, simply by failing to grasp the unique quality of Paul's personality. Paul moved across the room. Connor looked up, his fragile jaws munching. Paul said, "Suppose through your telescope you saw a big star heading right for the earth, what would you do?"

Connor wolfed another chunk of cheese. "I see them every night. Dozens of them. By the time they get here we'll be gone."

"Suppose doom was imminent."

Connor shrugged. "I'd take up ballet, something serious. Astronomy is a frivolous subject. All astronomers are frivolous. I'm frivolous. The most serious people in the world seem to be baseball players." He looked at Paul's highball. "Where's the booze?"

"There's a bottle behind the refrigerator."

Connor stalked across the kitchen, poured himself three fingers, added an ice-cube and with a dour nod at Paul went out on the back porch. Paul heard his feet thumping up a back-staircase.

Paul returned to the living room. Ted Therbow and the woman in green danced. Paul studied her figure, which was quite presentable from the rear. But he could not expunge the memory of the pink gums. And the evening was still young. Behind him the door opened, and Ira Slavinsky bellowed, "Come in, come in!" A murmur. "Absolutely!… Jeff, I'm Ira. You probably know everybody here."

Paul looked around. Jeff was tall, blond, and handsome, except for his round brittle blue eyes. He wore a hound's tooth jacket, gray flannel slacks as neat and well-fitting as those of Jim Connor were soiled and baggy. Behind him stood a dark-haired girl in black, her eyes roving the room with an innocent sparkle of excitement.

They entered the living room; Paul looked into the girl's face, leaned a little forward. The miracle… Her eyes met his, passed on. Half of a miracle at any rate.

Slavinsky led the newcomers to the far side of the room. He spoke to Jeff while the girl continued her scrutiny of the other guests. Her gaze came to Paul; then, just as her eyes met his Jeff spoke to her, and she turned to Ira Slavinsky.

Paul stood still and stiff. He looked at her left hand. No ring. Her age seemed to be nineteen or twenty. She was half an inch taller than average, slim and resilient; her hair was short, dark, rich. In her face Paul saw everything he needed to know. He choked with a longing which had in it nothing of lust. She was gallant, perfect; she represented something words could not express, emotions which never had been named. Could she not feel his presence, the pressure of his mind? Jeff led her casually to a chair. He asked her what she wanted to drink, then sauntered off to the kitchen.

Paul started forward, halted. He was frightened. Suppose she giggled or chewed gum or smelled badly? He drained his highball, set down the glass.

He crossed the room, seeing only the girl; the rest of the room was a blur.

She noticed him, she watched him approach. When he bent over her, she looked up with an indescribably charming half-smile.

"I want to talk with you," said Paul. "We'll have to dance, or we'll be interrupted."

She seemed puzzled in the faintest degree. For a moment she hesitated, looked toward the kitchen. "It's crowded," she said. Then she rose to her feet and faced Paul. They were dancing, amid the noise and shuffle.

She had not giggled, she chewed no gum, she was fresh as a meadow. Paul halted his first rush of words. She would find them incomprehensible; his intensity would alarm her. He spoke. His words penetrated her ears; he tried to freight them with far more than their literal meaning. "My name is Paul Gunther. What's yours?"

To a certain extent he had succeeded. She drew back a bit, examined him. "Barbara Tavistock."

"You're not married or engaged?"

"No." She looked at him even more searchingly. "Why do you ask?"

"If I told you," said Paul, "you might think me strange. Or, far worse, intoxicated."

She had become interested in him. She felt no fear of intensity. There was a queer tilt to her head which might signal an equal intensity in herself.

"Very well," said Paul. "I've fallen violently in love with you. When I saw you walk through the door."

She was considering. "Flattering. Unless it happens often."

Paul shook his head.

"I've never had this happen before," said Barbara Tavistock. "I don't quite know what to tell you."

"Perhaps you've fallen violently in love with me?"

She shook her head. "I hardly know you. In fact I don't know you at all. And you *have* had a lot to drink."

Paul fought back resentment. There was not to be the miracle then. "I've been drinking," said Paul. "No question about that. And why? Because it clarifies the mind. I understand the incomprehensible; I can see behind the veil, the eyes of Destiny shining..."

Barbara pursed her lips quizzically. Careful, thought Paul; it's no miracle; she can't instantly discard the values of her background and accept yours. He said in a light voice, "Unluckily I'll have forgotten everything tomorrow."

She was reassured. Jeff came in from the kitchen with highballs. He frowned when he saw her dancing, held up her highball by way of a signal. Barbara nodded.

Paul said, "Who is he?"

"Jeff Pettigrew. He's in the real estate business," said Barbara. "What do you do?"

There was already intimacy in their conversation. Paul said, "I'm a social worker. But that's not important. Basically—well, I believe in Life with a capital L. I want to make each moment of it significant. Then when I die I can tell myself, I've done as well as I could with this life."

Barbara looked at him slantwise. She hesitated, then said, "I feel the same way."

Paul felt a great throb of excitement. A juncture of their minds! The miracle, whole and complete! He said huskily, "Let's leave here. Let's go off by ourselves where we can talk!" But he knew he had made a mistake. Barbara Tavistock smiled coolly. "Even if I wanted to, I couldn't. I came with Jeff Pettigrew."

The music stopped. Barbara said, "It's been interesting talking to you."

The miracle had splintered into dismal little fragments. Too fast, too much, too soon. Paul said formally, "Thank you for dancing."

He went out into the kitchen, pushing blindly through the drunk and the half-drunk. The bottle behind the refrigerator was empty. Paul poured a glass of red wine from a gallon jug. He took a quick gulp, and cursed himself. Then he sat down at the kitchen table, shut out the voices, the noise of people coming and going.

He stared into the crimson depths of the wine, tilting the glass; the velvet disk swayed back and forth. The miracle required help, so much was clear. He had made a beginning; now he must consolidate, or Barbara Tavistock would dismiss him from her mind, think him no more than an impetuous drunk.

He rose to his feet, swaying a trifle. First, thought Paul, one or two questions to Ira Slavinsky, who might be prevailed upon to make a formal introduction.

He went out into the hall. The air was fetid. Faceless bodies leaned against the walls, lost in conversation or love-making.

Paul pushed past into the living room. The music played softly to the empty dance-floor. The peak of the party had passed. The guests were relaxed, mellow, drunk. Paul glimpsed Jeff Pettigrew leaving by the front door. The door closed behind him. Paul searched the room. No Barbara. Hesitantly he went out on the porch, and saw Jeff Pettigrew and Barbara cross the street to a new Chevrolet hard-top. They stood on the sidewalk before entering the car. Maple trees along the sidewalk shadowed them. Paul thought that they kissed there in the shade.

His throat lumped, his ears burned: shame, fury, humiliation, grief.

He swung back into the house. She had not waited to see him again. What of the miracle? Paul sneered. He'd made a fool of himself. But he wasn't done yet. He would have her, she would be his, and she would know hurt as deep as the hurt she had caused him. Savagely Paul searched the living room for the woman in green. She was gone. Ted Therbow also was nowhere to be seen.

Paul went to the kitchen, poured out another glass of wine. He took it back into the living room, found a seat on a studio couch. Beside him sat the astronomer Jim Connor. He closed his eyes as Paul turned to speak to him. The words caught in Paul's throat. Painfully he rose to his feet, stood glaring down at the placid form. Then turned on his heel, went to the front door, departed the house.

He crossed the street to his car, flung himself into the front seat, sat gripping the steering-wheel. Where to go, what to do now? Nowhere. Nothing. Paul cursed under his breath. He stopped short, laughed bitterly. What a fool he was making of himself. Weak, wavering, featherheaded, hysterical. He turned, reached over into the back seat for his briefcase. He brought it into the front, opened it. From among the reports, applications, forms, schedules and booklets, he brought forth a black leather-bound notebook.

Paul switched on the map-light. Slowly, almost reluctantly, he opened the notebook. He turned the pages until close to the back he came upon the words printed boldly:

CREED AND TESTAMENT OF FAITH

—— • ——

Seven years before, at the age of seventeen, he had awakened in the middle of the night. As he lay staring into the dark the meaning of time, the universe, his existence and his fate came clear to him. The sense of revelation was wonderful and terrifying; he stumbled to his desk and there scribbled the *Testament of Faith*. Thoughts out-raced his flying fingers, he wrote in an agony of apprehension that the illumination would fade, to leave him staring at a half-filled page.

The next morning he dared not read what he had written. He folded the 'Testament', tucked it in a place secure from the curiosity of his mother. Not until a month later, again at midnight, did he bring out the 'Testament'. He read it swiftly; it rang like a gong. Here was Truth. He read it more slowly, then copied it, and carefully derived a set of corollaries which he appended as 'Articles'.

Across the years Paul rarely read the 'Testament', for a variety of reasons. Tonight he read it with a renewal of exaltation: nothing could discourage him, nothing could divert him from his goals!

Headlights flickered in the rear-view mirror. A car parked across the street: a pale-blue Chevrolet hard-top. From the car jumped Jeff Pettigrew, then Barbara. They returned into the house, carrying a paper bag. Apparently they had only gone out to buy liquor.

Paul laughed: happy triumphant laughter. Such was his power; how magnificently the 'Creed' had forced the hand of Destiny! He crossed the street to the pale-blue hard-top, looked along the sidewalk. No one in sight. He opened the door, reached inside, pulled at the hood-release.

Jeff Pettigrew, driving with Lieutenant George Shaw along Lily Street, condensed his relationship with Paul into a few sentences: "I actually don't know Gunther too well, ran into him at a party or two. He took a shine to the girl I was going with, and we had a bit of a difference there. After he found I worked down here in his own bailiwick, we had lunch together a couple of times." He stopped the car, pointed to an ugly gray two-story house, isolated on the corner beside an empty lot. A sign staked into the dry yard read:

FOR SALE
by
McAteel Realty

"It doesn't look like much of a house," said Shaw. "What's the price?"

"Well," said Jeff, "the owner is asking thirty-five five. He might go as low as thirty if he got the right deal. It's been up a long time."

Shaw surveyed the house skeptically. "What would Gunther want with a place like this?"

"This isn't so bad," said Jeff breezily. "If a man spent a little money modernizing—new kitchen, new bathroom, wall-paper—he could turn a nice profit. I suppose that's what Gunther had in mind. In fact he told me as much."

Shaw grunted. "Let's take a look inside."

"We'll have to go around to the back."

In a central hall, at the foot of the stairs leading to the second floor, they found Paul Gunther, his arms spread wide, his throat cleft open in a great raw red valley. Blood flooding the linoleum floor had congealed into dark red paint.

"This is a mess," said Shaw. He looked around at Jeff Pettigrew who stood back in the hall, face the color of soap. "You go call headquarters. Ask for Inspector Morrissey. I'll wait here."

Chapter III

Lillian Gunther

Neil Hubbard lived in Bayview Highlands, a new subdivision twenty miles south of Oakland. If he left the office at five he almost instantly became wedged into the jam of rush-hour traffic and arrived home at six. If he delayed until five-thirty, the traffic had thinned and he still arrived home at six. So at five minutes after five, Hubbard sat at his desk studying a catalogue published by the Gloriana Health-Tone Equipment Company of Santa Monica. For several months Hubbard had wanted a rowing machine, several models of which were illustrated in the catalogue. Hubbard considered all of them, but his eye kept returning to the most expensive—the 'Supreme'. He wondered if the cost were justified by such special features as were embodied in this device: adjustable stirrups, Silvalloy frame, solid oak seat, stroke-counter, hemispherical trundle-arms, tension springs of finest Swedish steel. Hubbard pursed his lips. The medium-priced machine, the 'Deluxe', though not as handsome, probably performed as well. The low-priced 'Standard' model appeared inadequate even in the illustration, and Hubbard wasted no time with it. He frowned at the price of the 'Supreme', and turned to the page advertising wall-weights. No need to buy them, of course. With two pulleys, sash-weights and thirty feet of rope he could build his own wall-weights... Hubbard returned to the rowing machines. The 'Supreme': a fine professional-looking piece of equipment... The telephone rang. Hubbard lifted the receiver. "Hubbard speaking."

George Shaw identified himself. "We've located your man Gunther."

"Well, well!" said Hubbard. "Where has he been?"

"He ran into trouble. I'm sorry to say he's dead."

"Good heavens! Is he — is he — where is he?"

"Can you wait a few minutes? I'd like to ask some questions."

"Certainly," said Hubbard in a muffled voice. "Of course."

When Shaw arrived with Detective-Sergeant William Gaston, Hubbard was standing beside Paul Gunther's desk, looking uncertainly into the top drawer. The long office was almost empty; perhaps half a dozen social workers sat at their desks, typing or dictating into recording machines.

Hubbard raised his head; Shaw approached him. "You're Mr. Hubbard?"

Hubbard nodded, gingerly shook hands. Shaw looked inquiringly at the desk beside which they stood. "Is this —"

"It's Gunther's." Hubbard pointed. "Those are his files."

Shaw frowned at the open drawer. "You haven't disturbed anything?"

"Oh no. No indeed." Hubbard shook his head. "I really don't know why I came out here. The thing is so sudden, so tragic…" He made a helpless gesture. "What happened?"

"I don't know," said Shaw. "We found Gunther in a vacant house, his throat cut. Apparently he went there of his own accord. Who, why, how — we don't know."

Hubbard chewed at his lower lip. "This Mr. Big business — do you think it got him into trouble?"

"I don't know. It's certainly possible." Shaw picked up the two letters which lay to the side of Paul's desk, opened them. The first contained the bank statement and a number of canceled checks. The statement showed a balance of $924.86. Shaw skimmed through the checks, replaced them with the statement into the envelope. The personal letter Shaw read through without comment. He replaced both letters on the desk. "With your permission Sergeant Gaston will look through Gunther's papers."

"Certainly," said Hubbard. "I'm sure you'll find nothing but office business — but by all means look." He asked tentatively, "I suppose Paul's mother has been notified?"

"Not yet. After I leave here I'll run out and see her. She lives in Berkeley, I think you mentioned."

"I'll give you her address," said Hubbard. He added in a dismal voice, "I suppose I should go out with you."

Shaw glanced at him curiously. "If you feel that you should."

"The least I can do," muttered Hubbard. "My duty... Partly my responsibility, damnable business..." He gave his head a furious shake. "Foolish for me to feel the way I do, I suppose..."

Shaw made no response. Hubbard turned, led the way into his office. He motioned Shaw into a chair, seated himself behind his desk. "I'm just commencing to grasp the implications of all this," he said bitterly. "Publicity, notoriety..." He dropped the Gloriana Health-Tone catalogue into a drawer. "We work hard to maintain a favorable public image; you'd be surprised what it does for us. And now..." Words failed him.

"The police have the same problem." Shaw brought out his notebook. "How long has Gunther worked for you?"

Hubbard pulled at his chin, frowned. "Approximately three years. Tomorrow I can find out exactly, if it's important. I'll have to admit that I can't tell you very much about Gunther. Over a hundred people work here and there's considerable turnover. I simply don't have time to know the social workers well. However —" he hesitated.

" 'However'?"

Hubbard smiled ruefully. "It's not very much. I was about to say that I could hardly avoid noticing Gunther; I've been irritated by him many times. His attitude toward me, toward his work — I'd call it condescension. Contemptuous amusement."

"If he felt that way why did he stay?"

Hubbard straightened a pencil so that it lay parallel to the edge of the desk. "We have all kinds of people working for us. A college degree is the basic qualification, and many people who find other kinds of work uncongenial — well, misfits is too strong a word. Let's say that they're people who dislike business routine, or who are simply unsuited to a job where they've got to make money for the boss. Our work is fairly loose, although I think that under the circumstances we manage efficiently. In reference to Paul Gunther I doubt if he were dedicated to welfare work. I think he simply enjoyed the flexibility of his job."

"I see. How much did he make?"

"Eight hundred and thirty dollars a month," said Hubbard primly. "In accordance with our schedule."

"Now, back to last Friday. We notified you of this 'Mr. Big' situation. As I understand it, you called in Gunther; he informed you that he had a source of information in this regard. Right?"

"Hm…'Informed' is perhaps too strong a word. 'Hinted' might be better."

"Do you remember his exact words?"

Hubbard shook his head. "No. I believe that he said he'd ask around and very possibly might strike on some information. His attitude was more meaningful than his words."

"I see. Is it possible to learn where Gunther went Friday, who he called on?"

Hubbard blinked. "The information would be noted on Paul's case-sheet, which he'd carry in his briefcase." He drummed his fingers on his desk. "He was killed when? Has that been settled yet?"

"Late Sunday, so we estimate, perhaps Sunday evening."

"I see… He'd hardly be carrying his briefcase with him. His home address —" Hubbard made a fluttery, rather meaningless gesture.

"Has he friends in the office who might know where he lived?" asked Shaw.

"It's certainly possible."

"Well, that can wait till tomorrow. Now I'd better visit his mother." Shaw grimaced. "The hardest part of this whole business."

Hubbard said in a subdued voice, "I'd better go with you. It's my duty, to use an old-fashioned word."

"No need, Mr. Hubbard, unless you want to."

"I don't want to, Lord knows." Hubbard wavered, then rose to his feet. "I'll go."

"Just as you like." Shaw went to where Gaston sat at Paul Gunther's desk. "When you leave, bring those two letters. Anything else of interest?"

Gaston shook his head. "Nothing at all."

"Come out here first thing tomorrow, locate Gunther's friends, if any. Somebody must know his home address. It's not Orange Street; try for something better."

*

With Hubbard hunched beside him, Shaw drove north beside the gray-green bay. The sun dipped low over the Pacific, burnishing the towers of San Francisco, striking sparks from windows high among the Oakland hills. Shaw said, "Tell me something more about Gunther. What kind of chap was he?"

Hubbard considered, and shook his head. "For a fact, it's hard to say. He had no grudge against himself; I imagine he spent everything he made on girls and liquor and car payments. He wasn't especially popular around the office — that irritating air of condescension again. I can't complain of his work, and his clients seemed to like him." A caustic note came into Hubbard's voice: "What with his own free and easy life, I suppose he wasn't too critical of what they did with their money. It's possible that some of our people lean over backward; they go into the client's home, click their tongues at drunkenness, sluttish housekeeping, things like that. Not Paul Gunther."

"He'd be a man black people might confide in?"

"Referring to this 'Mr. Big' affair? I think so. Naturally it's a sensitive subject and they'd never openly confess to fraud."

"It sounds reasonable enough." Shaw turned off the freeway, drove up University Avenue into the heart of Berkeley. At Oxford Street he bore to the left, into the dignified apartment and residential area to the north of campus.

Mrs. Lillian Gunther lived at 600 Halcyon Way, the Yvanette Arms: a U-shaped apartment building with a luxuriantly planted garden-court between its wings. Shaw parked the car, alighted with grim deliberation. Hubbard pulled at his coat, straightened his tie, joined Shaw. They passed through a wrought-iron gate into the garden, followed a winding path to the front entrance. Shaw inspected the row of name-plates, pressed a button. The door-buzzer sounded, they entered.

Mrs. Gunther's apartment was No. 303, to the front. Shaw pressed the door-bell; almost instantly the door was snatched open and the snub-nosed face of a small middle-aged woman pushed furiously through. "Shush! Go away. We can't see you today, no matter who you are."

Shaw stared, non-plussed. He put his big hand up just in time to stop the door from closing. "A moment, please. You're Mrs. Gunther?"

The round head shook, black eyes glared. "Mrs. Gunther's just received terrible news; she can't see anyone."

"I'm from the Police Department, ma'am. May I ask what is this terrible news?"

"Her son has just been found dead. She's lying down. Now will you please —"

"How did Mrs. Gunther learn of her son's death?" asked Shaw bleakly.

"I'm sure I don't know. And now, if you please —"

"I'm sorry, ma'am. I'll have to speak to Mrs. Gunther a moment or two."

There was wrangling in hushed voices; the woman insisting that Mrs. Gunther could see no one, Shaw stating that nevertheless and regrettably he must speak to her. When the woman threatened to call the police, Shaw reminded her that he in fact was the police, and that such a call would be futile. Finally from within came a sad weak voice, "Oh Miriam, it's all right. Do let them in."

Shaw and Hubbard walked gingerly into the living room. Drapes were drawn against the golden afternoon light, which nevertheless penetrated and suffused the apartment. The carpet was beige, the walls pale brown, the furniture smooth, careful and bland. Over the white marble fireplace, separated by a mirror, rather surprisingly hung a pair of stately deer heads. Mrs. Gunther, wearing a pale-green dressing-gown, lay full-length on the couch, even in grief a woman of presence and careful grooming. She was tall and slender; her hair was glossy lavender-white, her features spare and fine-drawn. A lady in the old-fashioned sense of the word, thought Neil Hubbard.

She raised herself to a sitting position. Her face was flushed, her eyes inflamed, her mouth crooked with strain. Shaw apologized for his intrusion. "We naturally feel deep sympathy for you."

"How could anyone be so horrible!" said Mrs. Gunther huskily. "To do to anyone what he did to Garnett!"

Shaw looked at her blankly. "Garnett?"

Mrs. Gunther drew her hand in front of her eyes. "You must excuse me; I'll try to compose myself."

"It's a terrible affair," said Shaw. "We're doing everything we can to apprehend the criminal, and I know you want to help us."

Mrs. Gunther nodded emphatically, and her voice trembled with emotion. "I'd do anything, absolutely anything, to punish such a person!"

"I'm glad to hear that," said Shaw. "You can help us a great deal by answering a few questions."

Mrs. Gunther lowered her head with a weary sigh. "Of course. Ask whatever you like. I'll answer as best I can."

"First, how did you learn of your son's death?"

Mrs. Gunther repeated the question, mouthing the words as if they were bitter. "How did I learn of Garnett's death? A girl telephoned me. One of Garnett's young friends. She seemed very excited. She had heard of this terrible thing." Mrs. Gunther moaned softly. "She called to disprove what seemed a fantastic rumor."

Shaw nodded. "Do you know this young woman's name?"

Mrs. Gunther shook her head uninterestedly. "Garnett mentioned her once or twice. Barbara something-or-other. Tapscott? I think that's it."

"Tavistock," murmured Miriam.

"Tavistock. That's the name. Barbara Tavistock."

Hubbard watched to see how Shaw would react to the name 'Barbara', but Shaw merely asked, "Did she say from whom she had heard this rumor?"

"A friend seems to have told her. She did not name him. Naturally I called the police, and the story was verified."

"I see. Mr. Hubbard here is director of the Welfare Department, Paul's superior—"

"I also wish to extend my sympathies, Mrs. Gunther. We'll all miss Paul—ah, Garnett—tremendously."

"Thank you."

Shaw said, "I think you gave Mr. Hubbard Paul's address: 1417 Orange Street, as I recall."

"Yes, I believe that I did."

Hubbard shook his head. "Someone's made a mistake, Mrs. Gunther. There's no such address."

Mrs. Gunther frowned in bewilderment. "I know it's the address he gave me. He wrote it himself." She turned to the little round woman. "Miriam, dear, would you be kind enough? My red appointment book."

Receiving the book, she turned limply through a hoard of envelopes, letters, cards, leaflets, folded papers. "Yes. Here." She examined an envelope. "1417 Orange Street."

"May I see it, please?" Shaw crossed the room, took the envelope. On the reverse side someone had written *Garnett — 1417 Orange Street, Oakland.*

"Garnett is Paul, of course?"

"His full name is Garnett Paul Gunther. I have always called him 'Garnett'."

"This is his handwriting?"

"He wrote it himself."

"Hmf." Shaw shook his head. "He made a mistake. Or he wanted to keep his real address a secret."

"That is absurd!" cried Mrs. Gunther. "Why would he have any secrets from me? After all, I'm his mother!"

"Has he ever mentioned anything you might consider a clue to his residence? A shop? A street? A theater? Any association whatever?"

"I'm afraid not. Tell me please, how does this all bear on Garnett's death? I just don't understand!"

"We're anxious to trace Paul's movements on Friday. The information would be noted on the papers he carried in his briefcase, and the briefcase is probably at his residence."

Mrs. Gunther nodded, leaned back on the couch, closed her eyes wearily. Miriam glared at Shaw, snorted indignantly; but Mrs. Gunther limply raised her hand. "It's not important, dear."

"It certainly is!" Miriam declared energetically. She swung toward Shaw. "I think you've troubled Mrs. Gunther sufficiently! She needs a sedative and sleep, not an inquisition! Don't forget that she's had a dreadful shock!"

"No, Miriam," said Mrs. Gunther. "I'd rather talk, if you can believe it. This terrible pressure grows and grows. Unless I talk, I feel that my head will simply split."

"Well, then, just as you wish."

"When did Paul — or Garnett, if you prefer — leave to set up his own residence?"

"Several months ago. In April, I believe."

"Why did he decide to move? Did you quarrel?"

"Of course not. Never. We lived a very even life. It's the old story, I suppose. I considered certain of Garnett's associations unwholesome, and he enjoyed this dreadful music which seems to be the vogue. Perhaps I'm old-fashioned... I must say, however, that we never quarreled, and I don't believe I interfered too much in Garnett's life. Naturally he made his little contribution toward expenses — not that I needed the money — but I feel it's so important to a person's self-respect to know that he's paying his own way."

"Of course. Exactly when did he move?"

"Let me think... Oh I'm so muddled. It would probably be — yes, April 20th..."

On April 18th, a Saturday, Paul bought a used guitar and a book of instruction. Returning home at four o'clock, he found his mother in the bathroom, her face smeared with a clay-like preparation containing royal jelly, lanolin and a number of other substances.

Paul sat down on the sofa, took the guitar from its case. Consulting the instruction booklet, he proceeded to tune it.

"Is that you, dear?" trilled Lillian Gunther from the bathroom.

"Yes, mother."

"What is that ringing sound?"

"A guitar. I'm tuning it."

"A guitar! Oh dear. I hope you're not planning to be serious again. You become so intense."

Paul made no reply. Presently the guitar was tuned to his satisfaction. He consulted the first lesson: CHORDS FOR THE KEY OF C. *Learn these chords carefully. First: C Major.*

Paul placed his fingers as the diagram indicated, strummed. C Major. So much for that. Next: G-7th.

His mother swept from the bathroom into her bedroom. Presently, wearing a pale green satin dressing robe she came into the living room. Paul looked up. "Going out?"

"Yes. To the Martinons' for cocktails. I'm sure you'd be welcome if you'd like to come."

Paul bent his head over the guitar, practicing the change from C to

G-7th. "No thanks, mother. The Martinons don't interest me particularly."

"Ursula will be there."

"She's a Martinon." And Paul studied the F Major chord.

Lillian Gunther did something with the muscles around her mouth which changed the entire set of her jaw. "A lovely girl. Wholesome. Well-read. So much poise. And very pretty."

"If you like the St. Bernard type." C Major, G-7th, F.

"Oh by the way," said Lillian Gunther. "Miriam came up today. She's been ordered to increase the rent ten dollars on every apartment. And food is becoming ever so expensive. I'm afraid we'll have to increase your contribution just a wee bit. Otherwise I just can't see how I'll come out even."

"Sure thing, mother. Whatever you say. You're doing more for me now than I deserve." C, F, G-7th, C.

"Garnett, please, for just a moment. I want to talk seriously to you."

"Of course." Paul lolled back on the sofa. Then he jumped up. "Wait till I open a can of beer. Like one?"

"No."

On whimsical impulse Paul hung the guitar on the antler of one of the mounted deer heads; Lillian Gunther gave an instant cry of protest. "Garnett, your father's trophies!"

"Sorry." Paul propped the guitar against the wall, went out into the kitchen. When he returned he found his mother sitting on the sofa, moving her jaw in quick little chewing motions.

"Now then," said Paul cheerfully, "here we are." He reached for his guitar. "Care to sing? I'll play accompaniment."

Lillian Gunther shook her head impatiently. "I worry about you, Garnett." She glanced at the guitar, averted her eyes. "You have a college education, such a wonderful potential, but you're not giving your best! I want to see you make something of yourself, but you seem so frivolous."

"Oh, I'm getting there," said Paul equably. "Slow but sure."

"Very slowly indeed. I've almost decided to speak to Mr. Martinon this evening. He could get you such a wonderful connection at Godfrey, Paulman and Smith."

Paul laughed. "Not on your life, mother! I'd be the world's worst stock-broker."

"But that's where the nation's future is! In stocks and bonds. Mr. Martinon has told me as much and he certainly should know."

"Perhaps. But not for me. I like a more varied existence. And as a social worker I fill a useful niche."

"Where does it all lead? Eight hundred dollars a month? I'm certain you could do better."

"I am doing better. By thirty dollars."

Lillian Gunther shook her head impatiently. "It's a position with very little prestige. You might as well be a truck-driver."

"I'd make more money if I were... But what's money?"

"You can afford to ask," said Lillian Gunther, "so long as you have your mother to provide a home for you. How could you manage otherwise? Your car, clothes, all the little nice things?"

Paul reached for his guitar, rubbed his fingers along the strings. "I've got plans, mother. I'm going to start saving. As soon as I accumulate a little stake, just watch my smoke. There's money to be made in real estate, if you're on the right spot at the right time."

Lillian Gunther shook her head. "This is all so visionary, Garry dear. Suppose you make a single wrong investment, and all your little nest-egg is wiped out? I don't want you to waste your entire life at this work. I know it's necessary, but — well, it's hardly the most dignified position in the world, is it? As you know, I have no race prejudice, but I'd find it very depressing to be thrown so much into the company of negroes."

"Not at all," said Paul. "Quite the reverse. I enjoy working among blacks. They have much more charm and vitality than white people. Their sense of humor is tremendous."

Mrs. Gunther curled her lip. "Sometimes I think you'd prefer to live among negroes than here."

Paul laughed in great good humor. "Something to be said for the idea."

"No doubt, Garnett. Don't think that I disapprove of your tolerance. It's admirable, of course, but I do wish you'd find a more promising position. I put you through college —"

"Now, mother, you know better than that. I borrowed the money from you. I've paid almost half of it back."

Lillian Gunther sat rigid on the couch thinking. It served no purpose becoming angry with Garnett; his response was apt to be no more than a chuckle. Sometimes she was not sure that she understood her own son! It was very hard indeed to get under his skin, and the attempt so tiring that she seldom tried it. If only Garnett would become interested in Ursula Martinon! She'd straighten him out. There was a girl to brook no nonsense. And that other girl: "Whatever happened to the sweet young lady you met at the Getmore's. Charlotte Corngill? Is that her name?"

"Nothing happened to her, so far as I know. Nothing at my hands, certainly."

"Now Charlotte is a girl I approve of, wholesome and decent."

Paul laughed. He began plucking guitar strings at random. "Mother, you're wonderful! Machiavellian old Mother! I know what you're up to. You want to cleave me to one of these bluff overgrown girl scouts, and let her make a good Republican out of me. It's impossible, mother. I vote the straight Anarchist ticket. Now you run along to your party, and don't try to out-drink Mrs. Martinon."

Lillian Gunther rose to her feet, walked gracefully to her bedroom. At the door she turned a glance over her shoulder, hoping for evidence that her counsel had fallen on fertile ground: a pensive expression, an anxious gesture that would call her back for further discussion. But Paul sat engrossed in the instruction booklet. As she dressed she heard him practicing.

Three days later Paul announced that he planned to move. "It's so far to work, Mother. I've found a very nice little place downtown — fallen into it really."

His mother's face became very still. Then she looked out the window, moving her jaws as if chewing a thread. "You'll be giving up a great deal, you know."

"It's about time I was living out on my own," said Paul. "I've sponged off you long enough. I know my contribution doesn't cover expenses. And how else can I sow my wild oats?"

"Just as you wish," said Lillian Gunther coldly. She swung away sharply, walked from the room, to convey the idea that Paul had hurt her far more deeply than her self-control allowed her to demonstrate.

*

Shaw and Hubbard returned to Oakland as they had come, along the Bayshore Freeway. Sunset was a half-hour past. The sky over the Pacific still glowed tangerine, orange, pale green, but dusk had settled over the bay, and the great cities along the shores had become areas of twinkling murk. How calm, thought Hubbard. How unreal! And somewhere off in the brittle, violet, blue, black crumble stood Mr. Big, with blood figuratively dripping from his hands... Hubbard frowned, pulled at his chin. He said tentatively, "Of course, we have no *proof* that Mr. Big is responsible for this business."

"At the moment it's the only lead we've got," said Shaw without interest. "We'll have to stick with it until something else develops."

"That's reasonable, of course," said Hubbard. "But on the other hand..."

Shaw turned him a questioning look. "On what other hand?"

"Naturally I'm anxious to keep the department in the background," said Hubbard. "In fact, if somehow we could omit all reference —"

"Difficult," said Shaw. "Here's how I see the situation. Gunther interviewed a group of people Friday. Presumably he made inquiries about Mr. Big, and at some stage along the line started something going. Sunday night he got killed. So, as a first step, I want to talk to the people Gunther saw on Friday."

Hubbard said in a dismal voice, "I don't know who they are. Paul would have noted their names in his reports — but we don't have the reports. They're in his briefcase."

"These people would be among his regular clients, right? And you know who they are?"

"There's over a hundred. We'd have to check the entire file."

"No way we could eliminate some of them? The people he hasn't seen for a while?"

"Not if you want to be thorough. Remember he went out to ask questions about Mr. Big. He might have visited almost anyone."

Shaw considered. "The people who've been cheating the Welfare Department would be most likely to draw the attention of Mr. Big. I don't suppose there's any way of pin-pointing these people?"

Hubbard shook his head glumly. "If we suspect anything of the sort, we investigate. If our suspicions are well-founded, we cut the guilty party off the rolls, and possibly prosecute. I must say that Paul was rather lax in this regard."

"'Lax'?"

"Lax, easy-going, careless with the Department's money. A fraudulent recipient naturally tries to deceive the social worker. If the social worker is alert he senses when everything is not as it should be. A man's clothes in the cupboard, too many empty bottles, suitcases, a new television set, sometimes the very behavior of a client will give the game away."

"In other words, the social worker does the checking, makes the recommendations?"

"More or less. We have special investigators, but their function is basically the location of absent fathers... I suppose I could split Paul's file among five or six of my people and have them check to see where Paul called on Friday."

"That would be very helpful."

A few minutes later Hubbard asked, "Did you learn anything from the house where Paul was killed? Fingerprints, things like that?"

"Nothing to speak of. We're making inquiries around the neighborhood. Something might turn up." Shaw pulled over to the curb in front of the Welfare Department. Hubbard got out, bade Shaw goodnight. He watched the tail-lights dwindle into the stream of traffic, then turned, went up to the big office on the second floor.

The janitor was at work, and the long line of fluorescent fixtures filled the room with an aquarium luminescence. Passing Paul Gunther's desk, Hubbard paused, went to the file cabinet. Listlessly he opened it, glanced along the rows of manila folders, certain of which displayed colored tabs: blue, red, green, yellow. Hubbard's broad forehead creased in perplexity. There was no official method for coding. Paul seemed to have created a system of his own.

Hubbard glanced through each of the three drawers, then went into his own office. He picked up the telephone, dialed. A voice responded. "Eunice dear," said Hubbard, "this is Neil. I've been delayed. A dreadful thing has happened... No... No, of course not... I'm on my way right now... I'm sorry, I had no opportunity to call before..."

Chapter IV

Barbara Tavistock

At nine o'clock the following morning Shaw parked his car at the rear of the main post office. He climbed up on the loading dock, showed his credentials, and was directed down a long gray-painted corridor floored with scarred linoleum.

He found his way to the sorting room, where a clerk pointed to a short gesticulating man, apparently in a stamping frenzy of rage. "Wild Waldo McKissick, he's the man you want to see."

Shaw approached the superintendent who whirled about to display a round pink face, a quivering black mustache. Shaw again brought forth his credentials, and made his wishes known.

The superintendent weighed the request carefully, squinting first at the ceiling, then at the floor, and came to a grudging decision. Signaling Shaw to follow, he set off along the central corridor, legs pounding, arms swinging. They passed a series of aisles, where men on stools flicked envelopes into pigeon-holes; then turning down one of these aisles, halted beside a slender black man with aquiline features and close-cropped hair. "Cope," said Wild Waldo, "this is Lieutenant Shaw, from the City Police. He wants to ask a few questions."

"Certainly, glad to oblige." Cope looked from Shaw to McKissick, back to Shaw. "What can I do for you?"

Shaw waited woodenly. McKissick stood like a bulldog, head thrust forward. Shaw turned him a glance of mild inquiry; McKissick spun around and walked quickly away. Shaw turned back to Cope.

"How long have you been on your present route, Mr. Cope?"

"Almost eight months now."

"And you work the 1400 block of Orange Street?"

"That's right, sir."

"I turned up a funny situation. No reflection on you, I'll say from the start. A young man we want to know something about gave the address of 1417 Orange Street as his home. There isn't any 1417 Orange Street. But mail might have come to him at this address. I wonder if you'd know anything about that."

With a subdued air Cope pigeon-holed two or three letters. He looked back at Shaw. "How far does what I tell you have to go?"

"It stops right here."

Cope exhaled in relief. "I haven't done anything wrong, but Wild Waldo, he's a great one for the book. Everything's got to be just so. But I'll tell you about 1417 Orange. Mr. Gunther, that's his name."

"That's right, Paul Gunther."

"He met me on the route one day, and gave me a ten dollar bill. He said, 'I made a mistake, Mr. Postman. I gave the wrong address to some people. They might write me at 1417 Orange, and there isn't any such house. So if I get any mail would you be kind enough to send it along?' I look at his ten dollar bill and think, why not? He could come down here, fill out a change-of-address card, and I'd get the card. It's like he's giving me ten dollars to fill out his change-of-address card. So I say okay."

Shaw nodded. "No harm done, so far as I can see. What forwarding address did he leave with you?"

Cope carefully pigeon-holed three more letters. He looked sidewise at Shaw. "I don't really like to give anything away. This Mr. Gunther, has he done something wrong?"

"Nothing I know of. He's dead, as a matter of fact. I'm trying to find where he lived."

"Oh... Well, I guess you'd better ask at the Welfare Office, on Fourth and Broadway. That's the address he gave."

Shaw's face became square and doleful in disappointment. "Did he get many letters?"

"No sir, maybe one or two a week." Cope's hand went hesitantly to one of the pigeon-holes. He pulled out a sheaf of mail, riffled through it. "There's nothing here."

"Is there anything else you can tell me about Mr. Gunther?"

"No, I'm sorry. I only saw him that one time."

Shaw returned the way he had come. He saw Wild Waldo McKissick at the other end of the room, but McKissick turned his back. Shaw found his own way to the street.

He sat in his car thinking, sorting out the jobs ahead of him. Hubbard could not yet have any information. He reached in his pocket, brought out the two letters which he had taken from Paul's desk. The bank statement, which he would check more carefully later, had yielded nothing of immediate urgency. The letter from Barbara Tavistock, on the other hand, was intimate, if disillusioned and bitter. If anyone knew Paul's address, it might well be Barbara Tavistock.

He drove to a gas station, parked, stepped into the telephone booth. The directory gave him a number; he dialed, and a girl's voice answered. Shaw asked, "May I speak to Miss Barbara Tavistock, please?"

"Just one minute, I'll see if she's up."

After a three-minute wait, a second, rather drowsy, voice spoke. "Hello."

"Miss Barbara Tavistock?"

"Yes."

"This is Lieutenant George Shaw, Oakland Police Department. If it's convenient, I'd like to call on you for a few minutes."

"Oh." Barbara Tavistock's voice was thoughtful. "About Paul Gunther, I suppose?"

"That's right."

"I can't help you very much."

"I'll have to talk to you anyway."

"Just as you like. I don't suppose you have any idea who did it?"

"Nothing definite. I'll be at your house in half an hour, if that's agreeable."

"Can you make it an hour? I'm just getting up."

Shaw telephoned the Welfare Department and was connected with Neil Hubbard.

"Good morning, Lieutenant," said Hubbard, his voice ringing with enthusiasm and vitality. "Glad to hear you're on the job. I've put eight men to checking out Paul's file; the sooner the better, eh?"

"Right."

"I should have a report this evening. If eight men can't go through a hundred names in a day, I'll finish the job myself."

"I'll call you late this afternoon, then."

"Fine and dandy. Anything new at your end?"

"Nothing particular."

"Did the neighbors around that house on Lily Street have anything to say?"

"No. We drew a blank there."

"Too bad. Maybe today we'll dredge something from the depths."

Shaw left the telephone booth. He drove along the shore of Lake Merritt, up tree-shaded streets into Piedmont. Flores Way led through a district of impressive old houses, towering oaks, sweeps of lawn and formal gardens. Number 888, on the corner of Mara Road, sat back from the street, concealed by a fence of weathered planks and a screen of foliage. Shaw parked in the street, walked through a gate, along a graveled path. A red-tiled roof came into view, then the rest of the house, a two-story building of timber and stucco, after that style known as Early Californian.

Shaw rang the front door bell. Barbara Tavistock, wearing a gray plaid skirt, a white blouse, a loose gray cardigan, opened the door.

Shaw appraised her, seeing a girl boyishly angular, with a cap of thick dark hair, a look of brooding intelligence. Her mouth drooped pensively, her eyes were long, shadowed with dark lashes.

"Lieutenant Shaw?" At Shaw's nod, she smiled faintly. "Come in, won't you?"

She led Shaw into a vast living room, massively beamed, walled with cream-colored plaster. The tiled floor was spread with Navaho rugs; the furnishings dark and heavy. Barbara led him to an aromatic old leather couch, and sat beside him, legs curled beneath her. "Mother's in Honolulu, Father's in San Francisco, Meg and I are alone in the house. Except for the help, of course. Meg's my younger sister."

"I see. And you're a student?"

"I go to Cal. My junior year." She studied him a few seconds. "You're investigating Paul's death, you told me."

"Yes, that's true."

Barbara laughed shortly. "Father won't approve of my talking to you. He's an attorney; I doubt if he'd admit that the sun rises. Personally, I don't have a thing to hide. I'd just as soon talk. Whatever you want to know."

Shaw leaned back. "Before I apply the third degree I'll explain the problem. We're trying to get a lead into what so far is a very puzzling case. I hope you can help me."

A girl of fourteen appeared in the archway, already as round and demonstrably female as Barbara. She wore white shorts, a pale blue blouse, white rubber-soled moccasins and stared with frank interest at Shaw.

Barbara said, "My sister Meg. She's on her way to play tennis — I think."

"If you want to get rid of me, why don't you merely say so?" Meg crossed the hall, flung open a closet, took out a tennis racket, departed.

"Spoiled brat," said Barbara. "I suppose I was too at her age. I suppose I am now. Well then, what did you want to know?"

"Everything you can tell me about Paul."

Barbara looked at him quizzically. "Where do I start?"

"Anywhere you like. Perhaps you can tell me where he lived?"

Barbara seemed surprised. "Is it a secret?"

"I don't know for sure."

"On Orange Street, in West Oakland. 1417 Orange Street."

"He doesn't live there. No one lives there. It's a fictitious address."

Barbara stared. "Are you sure?"

"Very sure."

Barbara considered. "In a way I'm surprised. In another way I'm not. Paul was quite odd."

"So it seems," said Shaw. "But then, who isn't?"

Barbara turned him a quick glance as if to re-assess him. She leaned back against the padded arm of the couch. "Paul was a man of the Renaissance: brilliant, clever, unprincipled. He lived as if he might die at any moment —" Barbara stopped short, looked in sudden concentration at Shaw.

"I know what you mean."

She took a deep breath, continued. "Paul was an atheist, deeply, fervently. I'm an atheist, and I'm disgusted by this current religiosity, but not with anything like Paul's zeal."

"Hmf... I'm surprised. I haven't had that slant on Paul before."

"What? The atheism?"

"No. The zeal. Everybody seems to consider Paul a debonair smooth type."

Barbara's look of brooding intelligence returned. "He was that too — sober. When he started drinking he'd change. Not necessarily for the worse. I met Paul at a party." Barbara laughed self-consciously. "He'd been drinking. I was with Jeff Pettigrew that night. I don't know if it has anything to do with his death —" she hesitated.

"Did Jeff have reason to resent Paul's attentions to you?"

"I'll tell you what happened, but for heaven's sake don't jump to conclusions. Jeff might very well have been annoyed, but he wasn't annoyed enough to punch Paul in the nose, so he couldn't have been annoyed enough to kill him."

Shaw nodded his head. "There's quite a difference, I agree. Tell me what happened."

A maid passed through the hall; Barbara called: "Emily, would you bring coffee, please?"

"Yes, Miss."

Barbara screwed up her forehead, looked down along her legs. "Incidentally, how did you learn about me? How did you know I knew Paul?"

"You wrote him a letter."

Barbara blushed. "Oh," she said faintly.

"Also Paul's mother knew of you."

"I see." She straightened the pleats in her skirt. "I was telling you about the party where I met Paul. It wasn't a very hip party — although certain people there probably qualified. I guess you'd call it a middle-class Bohemian group: graduate students, artists, writers, people connected with the University. I don't go with that crowd very much, mainly because of Father. He thinks they're all Communists and homosexuals. Anyway Jeff knew the fellows who gave the party. I forget their names, but they seemed nice enough." Barbara snorted with sour laughter. "Jeff is something of a stuffed shirt, and he thought this party was a lark, a slumming expedition. Of course it wasn't. The people there just had more brains than Jeff. Jeff went out into the kitchen to get us a drink; when he came back I was talking to Paul." Barbara smiled sadly. "I noticed Paul when I came in. He stared at me as if he knew me. I was puzzled, because I didn't know him. I thought he looked interesting — dark-haired, pale, just a bit dissipated, if you know what I mean ... Well, it developed that Paul had fallen in love with me at first sight." Barbara laughed. "Naturally I don't believe in that — not too much anyway. But I couldn't help but be interested. He's a very interesting person — he was, I should say." Barbara frowned, and Shaw saw that her eyes were wet and luminous. She shook her head angrily. "If I wanted I could feel very badly about Paul's death ... But I'm not going to."

"Why not?"

"For personal reasons."

"Well then — back to the party."

Barbara wiped her eyes with her sleeve. "Jeff went out to buy a bottle of liquor, and insisted that I come with him. He wouldn't leave me alone, for fear of heaven knows what. When we got back Paul greeted us like old friends, and Jeff was quite annoyed. He tried to put Paul in his place but this was a mistake, as Paul was much more clever at lifemanship ..."

They were sitting on the studio couch drinking Jeff's liquor, Barbara in the middle. Paul looked into the highball glass and watched the bubbles rise. He spoke in a hushed entranced voice. "To think that when I was younger — not so very much younger — I promised myself that I'd never drink, never drug myself. I felt that my mind, sober and clear, must be capable of everything a drunken brain could do." Paul shook his dark neat head in wonderment. "How a person learns, how a person changes."

Jeff said bluffly, "I learned young. I was drinking in grammar school. And in high school, big beer parties all the time. We had a club — the Condottiere, we called ourselves. Talk about boozing —"

Paul nodded. "Kids do all kinds of things in gangs. It gives them security, do things they'd be afraid to tackle alone."

"I tackle lots of things alone," said Jeff.

"You're the rare exception," said Paul. "We live in an age of fear. Fear of the future. If you could give everyone a choice of living now or a hundred years ago — well, we wouldn't have to worry about overpopulation."

"Which would you choose?" asked Barbara.

"Oh, I'd stay here. I'm not the empire-building type. Jeff would be better at it. Trailing Livingstone through Africa, fighting Comanches, dancing the can-can, driving the Golden Spike..."

"I'm happy where I am," said Jeff. He took Barbara's hand, squeezed it possessively.

"You're probably better off," Paul agreed. "You go back a hundred years, there's the chance you might marry your own grandmother. Then where'd you be? A social outcast." Paul frowned. He told Barbara, "It works either way. Suppose that Jeff is actually a man from a hundred years in the future, and that you're his grandmother —"

"Barbara," said Jeff grimly, "Let's dance."

"Dance?" asked Barbara. "To that?" She referred to the music issuing from the loud-speaker: contemporary jazz, feverish, involute, eccentric.

"Let's try," growled Jeff. "Let's do something."

Barbara arose and allowed Jeff to clasp her. They danced, without pleasure or facility. Jeff's face was compressed into peevish lines; Barbara thought he looked like an irascible child. "That guy bugs me," growled Jeff. "I wish he'd get lost."

Barbara yawned. "I'm tired."

"'Tired'!" exclaimed Jeff, with sudden energy. "The evening's just beginning! From here we're going up to my place for bacon and eggs. Maybe a nip from the pinch-bottle."

"Oh Jeff, I can't. My father would think the unthinkable if I came in too late. I'm still his little girl."

The music stopped; Barbara turned back toward the couch, Jeff followed. Someone put a different record on the turn-table: Ellington of the 30's. The music burst forth, strong and sweet and wild, asserting sets of absolute truths. Barbara strove to translate this certainty into words, to capture it forever... Impossible; the sense was inexpressible.

Paul stood before her. She knew he was about to ask her to dance. His pale face seemed an integral part of the sad-sweet instant; at this moment she would have yielded herself entirely. As Paul bent forward she felt Jeff stiffen. Before Paul spoke she shook her head, meeting his eyes. Paul smiled in a manner Barbara thought infinitely understanding (but which Jeff found condescending and insolent).

Paul sat down beside Barbara. Jeff said brusquely, "Ready to leave, Bobbie?"

Barbara sighed, closed her eyes. "We really should. But I love this music."

Jeff squinted knowingly toward the record player. "Sounds like Ellington."

"*Black and Tan Fantasy*," said Paul. "Recorded in the early 30's."

"Too much like a dirge," said Jeff. "Good music, but the new stuff is better. More modern. Take Stan Kenton, for instance. That band really talks. Works things Ellington never even thought of."

Paul shrugged. "Some people read Tolstoy, others watch television."

There was a moment of silence, then Jeff said in a peevish voice, "Just what did you mean by that crack?"

"Each to his own taste."

The needle fell into a new trace. Barbara turned to Paul.

"What's this one?"

"*Daybreak Express*. Recorded about the same time. Ellington's answer to *Pacific 231*. Or maybe Honegger was trying to cut Ellington. I don't know which came first."

"I don't have nearly enough records," said Barbara abstractedly. "I must get this."

Paul told her, "Don't buy anything I've got already."

Barbara turned him a glance of sardonic inquiry, but the corners of her mouth dimpled.

Jeff rose to his feet. "Come along, Barbara. Let's blow this joint. It's getting dull around here."

"Yeah," said Paul. "I guess it's time to move on."

"Goodnight, Paul," said Barbara.

"Goodnight."

Jeff nodded coolly. Across the room Ira Slavinsky held a red-headed girl in black leotards. Ferdinand Fergus was nowhere to be seen. Jeff and Barbara said goodnight to Ira and departed.

Paul finished his drink, followed leisurely. He stepped out on the porch. Across the street came the sound of a grinding self-starter.

Paul sauntered over to the pale blue hard-top. Jeff sat hunched in the driver's seat, head bent over the steering-wheel. Again he tried the starter. To no avail.

Jeff cursed heavily. "God-damn engine!"

"What's the trouble?" asked Paul.

"Flooded the carburetor."

"Let her sit a minute or two. Or you'll run down the battery."

Jeff grunted. Paul went down the street to his own car, a two-tone Mercury sedan, started the engine, pulled alongside Jeff.

R-r-r-r-r, went the starter. Silence. The headlights reflected back from the cool mist blowing in from the bay. Paul could see Jeff's face clenched in annoyance. Barbara leaned against the other side of the car, a delicate dark shape.

Jeff hunched forward. *R-r-r-r-r-r.* To no avail. The battery was running down. Paul waited. Jeff turned his head sideways. "Hey. How about a push? This thing's just flooded; if I can get her rolling..."

"Sure." Paul backed, moved into position. Jeff performed the ritual of getting out to watch the bumpers touch, jumped back into the driver's seat, waved his arm.

Paul eased the two cars out into the street. He accelerated, felt the strain as Jeff engaged his engine. He pushed a block, two blocks, then Jeff waved his hand out the window.

Paul stopped, Jeff jumped out. He was puzzled, as well as irritated. "I don't get a sound out of it... Can't figure what's wrong..."

"Got plenty gas?"

"Hell yes. Tank's full."

"Probably your coil shorted out."

Jeff nodded unhappily. "That's what it feels like. Ignition trouble."

"I'll push you home, if you like," said Paul. "Where do you live?"

"Out Spruce. Not too far. If I get home I can coast to a service station in the morning." He added bluffly, "Hope I'm not putting you out any."

"Glad to help," said Paul.

Through silent streets, with mist blowing past the street-lamps, went the two cars. Spruce Street lifted ahead of them into the Berkeley hills. Jeff gave a signal; Paul slowed. Jeff made a U-turn, coasted to a stop in front of a dark brown-shingled house overgrown with ivy.

Paul got out of the car. Jeff said heartily, "Thanks a hell of a lot fella. You really saved the day. Don't know what we would have done."

"Annoying thing to have happen." He looked to the sidewalk to where Barbara stood huddled in her coat. "Sure you're okay now? How'll you get Barbara home?"

"Oh, I'll call a cab. Nothing to that."

"I don't mind dropping her off; it's not far out of my way."

"Really not necessary, fella."

"Jeff," said Barbara, "I think I'd better get home. It's awful late."

Jeff stood furious and irresolute. He looked sharply at Paul, who said nothing. Jeff turned to Barbara. "I'm responsible for you. Paul here might be a sex fiend, you can't tell. It's my job to see you home safely."

Paul chuckled. "Takes one to know one... Well, you come along too. We'll jointly guard the maiden's virtue. Jump in, let's get going."

Barbara told George Shaw, "Jeff called me the next day. He said some kind of wire had been pulled loose — from the coil to the distributor, or something similar."

"Did he blame Paul?"

"No... not directly. But I suppose he did a lot of speculating."

"And after this you began going with Paul?"

Barbara became instantly serious. "Well, yes. You could call it that. Up to a few weeks ago, anyway."

"Mind telling me what happened?"

Barbara tilted her head to the side, looked at her hands. "I don't mind... But I don't quite know myself." She laughed self-consciously. "This sounds ridiculous — but Paul idealized me. It's hard to be a fairy princess. Especially when Paul went out with other girls on, let's say, a more realistic basis."

"Who were these other girls?"

Barbara shook her head. "I don't know." She flicked him a sidelong glance. "Really, that didn't bother me so much. But he assumed that I'd go out with no one else. That did it. He was an absolute ocean of masculine conceit."

"And so you broke up with him?"

Barbara moved uncomfortably. "We didn't exactly break up. But I began to feel awkward around him." She made a fluttering motion with her hands. "He expected such *odd* things of me! As if I were spun-sugar and lily-petals! I'm not really. And I met another man..."

"You liked this man better than Paul?"

Barbara laughed sadly. "I've never been really sure that I liked Paul."

Shaw thoughtfully drank his coffee. Barbara fidgeted. She was almost certainly holding something back. "During all this time you never visited Paul's apartment, or wherever he lived?"

"When I first knew him he lived with his mother, in Berkeley. I met her twice." Barbara paused musingly, as if she would say more. She compressed her lips, and proceeded. "Two or three months ago he moved — to the Orange Street address. I've never seen this place. According to you, it doesn't exist."

"It doesn't."

Barbara said wistfully, "I'm surprised when I think how little I actually knew about Paul."

"One other thing. When you began going with Paul, what of Jeff Pettigrew? Did you still see him?"

Barbara pursed her lips. "Not so much. In fact, not at all. His feelings were hurt."

"Did Paul ever mention 'Mr. Big'?"

"'Mr. Big'? Not that I know of. Who is he?"

"A racketeer in West Oakland."

"I'm afraid that's out of my territory."

"What of Paul's friends? Do you know any of them?"

Barbara reflected. "I don't think he had any."

Shaw finished his coffee. Barbara watched him quietly. Too quietly, thought Shaw; she wants me to leave. He rose to his feet. "If you think of anything else, you'll let me know?"

"Yes, of course."

Perhaps she would, perhaps she wouldn't. In the meantime there was no use pushing her. "Goodbye, Barbara."

"Goodbye, Lieutenant." She stood watching as he walked down the gravel path to the street.

*

The rest of the day Shaw roamed West Oakland, putting discreet questions, receiving very little information. The name 'Mr. Big' was known and respected. "He's a real bad man," said the bartender in Jack's Café. "Don't pay to mess with Mr. Big." As to names, addresses, circumstances and details, Shaw drew a blank.

Late in the afternoon he returned to headquarters. Sergeant Gaston had found nothing suggestive among Paul's papers; the technicians had drawn a blank at the house on Lily Street. The neighbors had noticed nothing unusual Sunday night.

The following morning Shaw presented himself at the Welfare Department, climbed to the second floor, walked the length of the main office, now alive to the vibration of typewriters, the hum of voices. He spoke to Hubbard's secretary, and was admitted to the inner office.

Hubbard had slept poorly. The skin of his broad forehead was mottled; the eyelids drooped across his eyes, the little pink mouth compressed and curled like a boiled prawn.

"Good morning," said Shaw. "What did you find out?"

Hubbard, definitely not in a good humor, opened his drawer, brought out a sheet of paper. "These people saw Gunther Friday, at the times noted. There may possibly be others, of course."

Shaw took the paper, glanced down the paragraphs, each headed by a name: Smith, Perkins, Cappo, Laverghetti, Bethea.

"The numbers after the names refer to what?"

"Merely file numbers."

"And 'District 22'?"

"Most of Gunther's cases are in District 22."

"Your men made no further inquiries?"

"No. They established only that Gunther had seen these people, at the times noted."

Shaw examined the list. "Might any of these people be defrauding the Welfare Department?"

"Any or all of them," grumbled Hubbard. "We're considered fair game."

"In that case Mr. Big might be victimizing any of these people."

Hubbard pursed his lips, shrugged. "Something else to consider: Gunther visited these particular five people, but he might have gone elsewhere for the information about Mr. Big."

"It's a good point," said Shaw. "I'll keep it in mind." He rose to his feet. "I'll make the rounds and see what they can tell me."

"I'll be interested in hearing how you make out," said Hubbard.

Shaw nodded noncommittally and took his leave. Hubbard opened his drawer and brought forth a box of raisins. His eye fell on the Gloriana Health-Tone catalogue. He snatched it up, threw it at the waste-basket. Eunice had vetoed the rowing machine, pointing out that ordinary calisthenics cost nothing and were equally invigorating... Hubbard sat eating raisins and glooming for a moment or two, then applied himself to his work.

Chapter V

Smith, Perkins, Cappo, Laverghetti

MRS. WILMA SMITH A-1392
2716-A Bainbridge Street
Oakland District 22

Age 38. Resident in Oakland 4 years, previous Chicago. Five children, three dependent. Claims no precise knowledge of husband's whereabouts. Believes he is 'insane', confined in asylum back east. (Chicago?)
Paul Gunther: 10 a.m. Friday

In the course of his work Shaw had frequent occasion to visit West Oakland, a sprawling district of slums and semi-slums, inhabited for the most part by low-income blacks. Those families of middle-class status had gone to join their white counterparts in Berkeley and East Oakland, with new-comers from the Deep South quickly pre-empting the vacated space. It was an area of contrast and paradox, social, moral, psychological; Shaw never came to West Oakland without a sense of adventure.

He drove along Eighth Street, past barbecue joints, haberdasheries, record shops, dingy theaters, churches of the Living Gospel, markets, taverns, pool-halls, all in a matrix of fragile old frame houses. Ahead were night-spots: Slim Jenkins, the Zanzibar, Club Marimba, Sunset Terrace, The Ritz Club, the Spot, Jack's Café — Shaw turned off to the right, up Bainbridge Street.

He drove three blocks and found 2716, a gray two-story house with a green asphalt shingle roof badly in need of repair. Through an open upper window limp lace curtains rippled to the breeze.

Shaw parked his car, alighted. A sign indicated 2716-A at the rear. He went around to the back, knocked at the door to an apartment evidently converted from a former basement. From within came the sound of television. He knocked again, more loudly, and succeeded in arousing a dog to hysterical barking.

The television went silent; curtains at a small pane in the door trembled. The dog became quiet at a mumbled command. Shaw felt a suspicious scrutiny, then the door was opened by a heavy-bodied woman in a blue chenille bathrobe. Her face was round, cartilaginous rather than fat; her skin deep brown, her lips heavy, purple, surrounded by bands of muscle. Examining Shaw she blinked sleepily. "What you want, mister?" She spoke in a tired bored voice, her manner off-hand.

"You're Mrs. Wilma Smith?"

The woman nodded slightly, looked over Shaw's shoulder.

Shaw introduced himself, displayed his credentials. The woman's manner took on a faint flavor of truculence. "I'd like to ask you a few questions," said Shaw.

"About what? I like to know before I shoot my mouth off."

Shaw remained polite. "I'm making inquiries in connection with the death of Mr. Paul Gunther."

Wilma Smith's shoulders hunched beneath the blue chenille. "I don't know any man that name." She turned to go back into her apartment.

"Paul Gunther was the Welfare Man," said Shaw. "He saw you Friday at ten o'clock."

The round face swung back in astonishment. "That boy dead? What happen to him?"

"He was stabbed."

Wilma Smith pulled back the corners of her lips in a wry grimace. "My, my, my, the things that happen!...Well, that's too bad. He was a nice boy, had some respect. You know who cut him?"

"Nothing definite," said Shaw. "That's why I'm here now."

Wilma Smith blinked suspiciously. "I don't know nothing about anybody getting cut."

"You've been paying Mr. Big," Shaw said gently.

"Who say that?"

"Never mind who said what. Are we going to do all our talking in this doorway?"

"I ain't gonna do no talking."

"Do you want to come down to headquarters?"

Wilma Smith's lips curled contemptuously. "I ain't saying nothing, 'cause I don't know nothing." But she moved aside and Shaw stepped past her into the apartment. The room was over-warm, crowded with furniture in ruffled pink slip-covers, but obsessively tidy, with every magazine, bit of bric-a-brac and framed photograph in exact position. Through a door Shaw glimpsed the kitchen, no less immaculate, the sink shining, the linoleum waxed and glossy. Wilma Smith was house-proud, and exercised her home-making instincts to the utmost.

"What you looking around for?" she demanded. "Ain't nothing here."

"Just looking," said Shaw. "Who's in the bedroom?"

"Nobody in the bedroom! What you talking about?"

"I want to make sure," said Shaw. "What I have to say to you is confidential. Open the door. Unless you want me to."

Wilma Smith stared at him, exuding a musk of rage and hate.

"I don't work for Welfare," said Shaw. "I don't care what you do in your spare time. If you've got a friend visiting you, tell him to leave. By the window if you don't want me to see him."

The door from the bedroom swung quickly open; a short bullet-headed man in a beige jacket and rumpled charcoal-brown slacks, his skin an exact match for the slacks, appeared. He marched across the living room to the door, out and away.

Wilma Smith glared silently at Shaw.

"Anybody else around?"

Wilma Smith snorted viciously, dropped her massive buttocks into a chair. "Wish you'd leave me be, mister," she muttered.

Shaw seated himself in a second chair. "Let's quit fooling. I want straight answers. If I don't get them, you're in trouble."

Wilma Smith rocked her head up and down stonily — obduracy rather than compliance.

"You like that Welfare check? If you don't help me find out who killed the Welfare Man, you won't see that check any more."

Wilma Smith was thinking. She said presently, "I don't want no trouble. Ain't my way to mess in somebody else's business."

"Whatever you tell me stays right here. First—how much are you paying Mr. Big?"

"I ain't paying nothing."

"How much?"

Wilma Smith shrugged. "You know so much, how come you don't know that?"

"I want you to tell me." Shaw hardened his voice. "You want to come along to headquarters and have me ask you down there?"

"I got chillun," cried Wilma Smith furiously. "You take me, what you gonna do about the chillun when they come home from school?"

"Somebody else can sweat that out. I'm interested in just one thing. Come on now, let's hear it. How much?"

Wilma Smith was silent, Shaw rose to his feet. "Don't say I didn't warn you."

"Ten dollars," she said sulkily.

"Ten a week, eh?"

She nodded. "I ain't paying him now."

"No? How come?"

"I got a letter—just yesterday." She reached over to the magazine rack, found an envelope. Shaw took it, withdrew a sheet of cheap white paper. The message was printed in capital letters:

SEND NO MORE MONEY.
MR. BIG

"Well, well," said Shaw. "This came yesterday?"

"That is correct."

Shaw examined envelope and letter, put them into his pocket. "What's Mr. Big look like? You know his right name?"

Wilma Smith shook her head. "I never did see him. I got a letter in the mail. It said how much I was supposed to pay, and told me where to send the money. Otherwise he'd tell the Welfare man about my husband living in."

"How'd he find out about your husband?"

"I don't know."

"When Paul Gunther was here Friday, did he ask about Mr. Big?"

She nodded. "I didn't tell him nothing."

"Where did you send the money?"

"To the post office. Box No. 4912. For Mr. Bigley."

Shaw learned nothing more. He rose to his feet. "I'm not passing on what you told me, it's not in my line. But you better straighten out. What you're doing is fraud. They find out they'll put you down in Santa Rita for a year or two."

Unexpectedly Wilma Smith began to cry. Between great gulping sobs she uttered phrases: "...money, all them bill-collectors...take my furniture...chillun a nice home..."

Embarrassed, Shaw found himself beside Wilma Smith, patting the burly shoulder. "Now then, you straighten out. Make your husband pay the bill-collectors. Don't do anything crooked; you don't want your children to be ashamed of you."

Wilma Smith sniffed, stared morosely at the rug. Shaw went to the door. "Goodbye."

Wilma Smith made no answer. Shaw departed and went to his car.

MRS. ELVANOR PERKINS E-2122
1646 Trumbull Street, Apt. 4
Oakland District 22

Age 24. Born in Los Angeles, three years ago moved
to Oakland with her husband, then employed as
construction laborer. Gave birth to triplets.
Husband couldn't stand noise of crying, etc.; deserted.
Wife thinks he went back to Los Angeles. Maybe
Bakersfield.
Paul Gunther: 11 a.m. Friday

Shaw drove the three blocks to 1646 Trumbull Street, an ancient mansion three stories tall, authentic Victorian in that detail which had survived the years. On the stoop sat two elderly women, a boy of sixteen. Two small girls, restless and frisky, played tag up and down the steps.

Shaw crossed the street. The group on the steps silently watched him approach. Shaw stopped in front of them, made a pretense of examining the address on an envelope. "Where is Apartment 4?"

One of the women pointed. "Jes' go up the steps. Mind the milk bottles. We don't want nobody hurt."

The other woman asked, "You lookin' for Mrs. Perkins? She ain't at home."

"She's up there," said the boy. "She came in just a bit ago."

The woman said no more. Probably figures me for a bill-collector, thought Shaw. "Thank you," he said and climbed the stairs. From outside the door to Apartment 4 he could hear baby-sounds; shrill yelps and outcries. Thinking of the husband, Shaw grinned. He rang the bell.

The door opened. Elvanor Perkins looked forth, slender and well-shaped, almost as tall as Shaw, a handsome woman by any standards. Her skin was a deep burnished bronze; her features were narrow, well-shaped. Elvanor Perkins had been drying her hair; it lay over to the right of her head, fanning up at a fantastic angle, a mass of black foam in the shape of a leaning candle-flame.

"Mrs. Perkins? I'm Detective Lieutenant Shaw of the City Police. May I have a few minutes of your time?"

Elvanor Perkins nodded without comment, drew back. Shaw entered the apartment, which was clean but by no means as tidy as Wilma Smith's. A play-pen occupied the center of the living room, in which three two-year-old children stood staring at Shaw: three little girls dressed in white, pink and pale green.

"Will you sit down?" Elvanor Perkins asked in a carefully neutral voice.

"Thank you." Shaw took a seat on the sofa, this one upholstered in a pleasant gray-green. On an end-table were copies of *Sepia, Vogue, Ebony, McCall's,* one or two motion picture magazines.

Elvanor Perkins seated herself across the room, watched Shaw expressionlessly. Shaw said, "I'm interested in what you can tell me about Paul Gunther."

"Paul Gunther?"

"He's the young man from the Welfare Office."

"Oh, him." Elvanor Perkins idly ran a comb through her hair. "I don't know anything about him."

"Paul Gunther was killed Sunday night," said Shaw. "His body was discovered Wednesday."

"Ooh!" exclaimed Elvanor Perkins softly. "Isn't that terrible! He was nice."

"We understand that he visited you Friday."

"Yes. About eleven o'clock. That's what I told the other man who asked. He didn't say anything about Mr. Gunther being dead."

The children were quarreling over a huge yellow rabbit. The girl in white pulled it from the girl in pink, who promptly set up a wail. Elvanor Perkins eyed her apathetically a moment, then said, "Be quiet, Sandra."

Shaw asked, "Did Paul Gunther have anything at all extraordinary or out of the way to say last Friday?"

Elvanor Perkins shook her head; the sheaf of dark foam shifted and waved. Absently she ran a comb through it. "Nothing to speak of. Just the usual: how are things going, did I hear from my husband?"

"Did he mention Mr. Big?"

Elvanor Perkins' eyes shifted here and there around the room, in the maddening fad of disassociation, intended to convey the idea: I'm much more interested in myself and my affairs than in you and your affairs. "Now that I think back, he did say something like that."

"What were his exact words?"

"Oh, he was just joking. Asking how much I was paying Mr. Big. I'm not paying anything. I wouldn't give anyone a cent, let alone that Mr. Big. He's the meanest man there is."

Shaw nodded. "I agree. I want to catch up with him."

Elvanor Perkins inspected him with vague interest. "You think he might have killed Mr. Gunther?"

"Possibly. We don't know for sure. Do you know anything about Mr. Big?"

"No." She shook her head. "Just what I heard from a friend. She was on welfare too, but she got herself a boy friend. The boy friend was living in, if you know what I mean. Well, that old Mr. Big found out, and he made her pay seven dollars a week."

"That's the way he works."

"Sandra! Delsey! Behave now. Let your sister have Ooky awhile. That's the rabbit's name," she told Shaw. "Ooky. They named him that themselves."

"Three cute kids," said Shaw. "I imagine they keep you busy."

Elvanor Perkins smiled. "I don't mind. I love 'em. But I'd sure like to be off this Welfare. That don't do my pride any good at all."

Shaw shrugged. "Sometimes it can't be helped. You've got to eat, and feed the kids."

"Yes, I know. If it wasn't for them..." She left the sentence unfinished. Shaw rose to his feet.

"Thanks very much, Mrs. Perkins."

"I don't see how I've helped you very much." Elvanor Perkins was soft and winsome; Shaw couldn't imagine any husband whatever wanting to run out on Elvanor Perkins. He said, "You're a name scratched off the list, and that's a help."

He returned to his car. Two down, three to go.

MRS. MARY CAPPO A-1255
1777 Juniper Street
Oakland District 22

Widow. Age 76. Born in Gadsden, Alabama, moved to Oakland to join son and daughter-in-law, both convicted last year of grand larceny, serving five to ten years. Mrs. Cappo has custody of five children, oldest sixteen.
Paul Gunther: 11:45 a.m. Friday

Mrs. Cappo was old, small, scrawny; she stood crouched in a habitual stoop; her hair was white, her skin black and lined with as many wrinkles as a cantaloupe. She was hard of hearing, and told Shaw nothing he wanted to hear. Shaw thanked her for her time, retreated to his car. Three down, two to go.

ANGELO AND CORINNE LAVERGHETTI E-2965
1542 Juniper Street
Oakland District 22

Ages 38 and 32. Corinne born in Dallas, Texas,
came to California during war, worked in airplane
factories in Los Angeles, where she met and married
Angelo, native and a professional musician in 1948.
Laverghetti, now crippled, immobilized from
poliomyelitis, can't blow his horn. Two children.
Paul Gunther: 12:30 p.m. Friday

The room was hot and smelled oddly. Medicine? Chemicals? Rotten wood? Mildew? Definitely the house was not clean. Angelo Laverghetti sat in a wheel-chair, spidery and full of malice, eyes darting back and forth. Corinne was an enormous woman, tall and fat, slow-moving, the very antithesis of Angelo. They listened gravely to questions, considered them carefully. Corinne answered economically. Angelo fairly spat out sentences. Shaw wondered. Drugs? Benzedrine? Marijuana? That smell — stale marijuana smoke?

The Laverghettis were uneasy. Angelo spoke too furiously fast, Corinne deliberated too carefully.

Shaw asked bluntly, "How much are you paying Mr. Big?"

Corinne turned him a slow careful look, made a stealthy involuntary movement. Angelo chattered in rage. "Mr. Big! What you talkin' about man? What Mr. Big? Jokes, jokes, jokes. You think I got money for Mr. Big?"

"You know who Mr. Big is?"

"I heard the name. So what. I hear lots of names. Now I hear your name. I ain't givin' you no money. I ain't givin' Jesus Christ no money, not if he comes crawlin' on his hands and knees."

Shaw surveyed the racks and shelves along the wall. "You've got quite a record collection here."

"Sure. Got to get some kicks. You like to dig a little music? Corky, throw on a couple sides."

"Man don't want to hear no music," said Corinne placidly.

Angelo screamed in quick fury, "I'm not asking for a sermon, I want some friggin' notes!"

Corinne patiently dropped a record on the turn-table. Her complexion was pale brown, cinnamon-color; Angelo's skin had the look of unbaked bread, the Mediterranean olive gone sunless. Shaw wondered about the children. How would they turn out? Where would their lives take them? He felt a qualm of melancholy. Angelo noticed. "What's the matter? Don't dig Miles? Corky, blow some of the Basie."

Shaw asked, "How well did you know Paul Gunther?"

"What'd he play? You mean that alto man, Paul Gunnarson?"

"No. Paul Gunther, the Welfare Man."

"Oh, him." Angelo screwed up his agile face. "He'd drop by. We'd pass a few words, play a tune or two."

"He's dead," said Shaw.

"Oh? Too bad." Angelo raised a skinny claw-like hand. "Listen to this wailin' band!"

"Did Paul Gunther ask you about Mr. Big?"

"Maybe so." Angelo frowned and asked fretfully, "Is it important?"

"We'd like to find who killed him."

"Bah. He's dead. Let him rest in peace. Corky, pour us a couple beers."

"Ain't no more beer."

"Well for Chrissakes, hustle some! Music and no beer? That's like flying to Mars with the gas tank empty."

Corinne placidly went into the bedroom. "Well, so much for psychology," said Angelo.

Shaw said, "I'm not interested in your private affairs —"

"Because I married a jig? Mellow, man, real mellow. You'll never know till you try it."

"I'm talking about Mr. Big."

"He's nowhere, chum. Forget him."

"As I say, I'm not interested in putting you on the spot. Nothing you tell me goes any farther. I want to know, first, are you paying Mr. Big? If so, how much? How do you get it to him? Do you know the man personally? Don't forget, if I can put Mr. Big away, you won't be paying him."

"The answer is no," said Angelo. "Nix, Nyet, Nein. I don't know him from Alexander the Beat. That's the story on Mr. Big."

Shaw rose to his feet. Somewhere, somehow, money was coming into the house, from a source other than the Welfare check. Records, high-fidelity equipment, carpet on the floor, new television, diamond ring on Corinne's finger. To protect his income, Angelo paid off Mr. Big. Pushing dope, thought Shaw. Possibly an importer. He could hardly return into the open air fast enough.

Four down, one to go.

MRS. VIRGINIA BETHEA E-1882
2707 Van Buren Avenue
Oakland District 22

Age 49. Born Choctaw, Mississippi, arrived in Oakland 1932. Husband, Si Bethea, deserted last year, leaving her with two minor children. Si Bethea reportedly seen around town.
Paul Gunther: About 2 p.m. Friday

One to go. Shaw drove out Ninth Street in a neutral frame of mind, neither encouraged nor discouraged. As he reckoned it, only two significant facts had emerged from the morning's work: first, Mr. Big's post office box address; second, the letter received by Wilma Smith directing that no more money be mailed. The second fact seemed to cancel the usefulness of the first. After the death of Paul Gunther Mr. Big apparently was going as far underground as possible. Almost certainly he would not drop by the post office for his mail.

Shaw turned down Van Buren Avenue, drove slowly until he found a house number: 2544. Two blocks to 2707. Shaw's pulse beat in sudden excitement. Two blocks ahead Lily Street intersected Van Buren Avenue.

Shaw parked in the middle of the block. From the car he could see 2707 Van Buren Street, a two-story house, light green with dark green trim, crowned by an eccentric high-pitched roof. A pair of palm trees grew in the yard, which was delineated right and left by a tall hedge.

Directly across the street gaped an empty lot, with three or four stacks of rotting lumber to indicate the site of a demolition. Beside the empty lot, facing toward Lily Street, stood the old gray house where Paul Gunther had been killed.

Coincidence?

Perhaps. Perhaps not.

Shaw got out of the car, walked slowly toward 2707 Van Buren, his mind twisting and turning. But best not to speculate before he had a few facts.

He entered the yard, passed between the palm trees, climbed the steps to the porch. On one side was a lawn-swing with faded orange and green cushions, to the other a litter of comic books.

Shaw went to the door, rang the bell.

Chapter VI

Virginia Bethea

Inside the house a buzzer sounded. After an interval the lace curtain over the peep-hole quivered and the door opened. A girl of seventeen, skin the color of taffy, stood in the doorway, wearing a short-sleeved black sweater over leopard-print leotards. She had a wise merry little face with a snub nose, short hair carefully straightened and dressed after some shaggy modern fashion. Shaw asked, "You're not Mrs. Bethea?"

"No," said the girl pertly. "I'm Miss Bethea, and that's pronounced 'Bethay'. To rhyme with 'death-ray'."

"Is your mother at home?"

"You mean my step-mother? That's Vinnie; she's just back."

"I'd like to speak to her," said Shaw. "May I come in?"

Someone from inside the house called a question, the girl tossed an answer back over her shoulder: "Just a man. I don't know who he is." She looked back at Shaw. "You selling something, Mister? We don't need anything."

"I'm Lieutenant George Shaw, City Police."

The girl licked her lips and looked past Shaw toward the house on the corner. "You come about that killing across the street?"

"Partly. Do you know anything about it?"

"Not a thing. We just see the ambulance and the police cars, that's all we know. It's not nice, things like that so close."

"No," said Shaw, "I suppose not. May I come in?"

The girl stood back. Shaw stepped after her into the usual entry hall.

From behind a closed door came a harried voice. "Gally? Who you talkin' to?"

"Just a man. He want to see you."

There was the sound of a flushing toilet; the girl took Shaw into the living room. "Won't you please sit down? Vinnie'll be here in a minute."

"Thank you." Shaw seated himself on a worn green sofa. The girl stood uncertainly in the middle of the room, looking at Shaw, then quickly averting her eyes. Shaw noticed the vaguest hint of thickness about her middle: pregnancy?

Against the wall stood a suitcase with a black patent-leather carrying-bag leaning against it. "Going traveling?" asked Shaw.

Gally wrinkled her nose in scorn. "That old junk ain't mine. It's Vinnie's. She's just come back from San Jose."

"I see."

Conversation came to a halt. Shaw examined a framed photograph on the table at his elbow: Gally's high school graduation picture. Her skin was chalky, her smile synthetic; her hair like a wig. Absent was the impish charm, the raffish vitality.

"Don't pay attention to that picture," said Gally suddenly. "I look a mess."

Into the room came Vinnie Bethea, a tall woman coffee-dark, thin at the shoulders, broad at the hips. Her face was bony, her features prominent and poorly proportioned: nose like a rock, eyes small and nervous with eyelids puckered down at the corners, her lips taut over protuberant teeth. Vinnie Bethea was hardly beautiful, but she was nevertheless a woman of vanity. Her hair was coiffed intricately, and shone a suspiciously glossy jet-black. She wore several rings, a double string of amber beads, ear-rings in the shape of a yellow flower.

Shaw rose to his feet as Vinnie Bethea came into the room, reintroduced himself: "I'm Lieutenant George Shaw of the Oakland Police Department, Mrs. Bethea. I'm making inquiries into the death of Paul Gunther—"

Vinnie shook her head. "We don't know nothing about it, Mr. Lieutenant. There's already been a policeman here asking what we knew. I tell you what I told him: we don't know nothing!"

Shaw nodded gravely. "I see. Perhaps you'd answer a few questions?"

"Certainly, Mr. Lieutenant, I certainly will, if it helps out law and order, cause that's what we want around here."

Gally snickered; Vinnie threw her an indignant glare. Gally jerked her shoulders, sauntered from the room. Vinnie turned back to Shaw. "It's not that I don't want to help you, Mr. Lieutenant, I just simply don't know nothing."

Shaw resumed his seat. "You knew Mr. Gunther was dead, of course?"

"Oh yes. We saw the commotion over across the street and then it came out in the paper today."

"You know that Mr. Gunther was the man from the Welfare Department?"

Vinnie nodded. "I believe that he was. So they say."

Gally returned to the room, eating a banana. She leaned against the wall, one leg provocatively twisted to the side.

"I understand," said Shaw, "that Paul Gunther called around here Friday."

"Oh yes," said Vinnie primly. "Every month we saw him. You know my husband just took off and left me flat. I guess it's no secret, but I can't help it. Lots of other folks is in the same bad fix."

Shaw agreed politely. "And you noticed nothing unusual around here Sunday night?"

"Not one thing, Mr. Lieutenant. Not a single thing."

"You're sure? No lights in the house that night?"

"I'd have noticed for sure. Nobody wants to live in that old place; nobody with any respect."

"Poof," muttered Gally under her breath. Vinnie ignored her.

Shaw asked, "When Paul Gunther visited here Friday, how did he act? Was he nervous? Any different than usual?"

Vinnie hesitated, looked toward Gally, who examined her fingernails. "No," said Vinnie, "I guess he was about like always."

"Did he ask you if you'd been troubled by Mr. Big?"

Vinnie blinked. "Who you say? Mr. Big?"

Shaw nodded. "If you know anything at all about this man, please tell me. I want to catch him, and put him away for a long time."

Vinnie Bethea shook her head nervously. "Now, Mr. Lieutenant, don't go asking about things I don't understand."

"You've never heard of Mr. Big?"

Vinnie Bethea glanced again toward Gally, who daintily nibbled the last of the banana.

"Maybe it would be easier," suggested Shaw, "if you just told me everything you know."

"She don't know nothing," said Gally.

Vinnie Bethea swung around in fury. "Maybe I do, maybe I don't. And what you doing stuffing your greedy face with them bananas? There's lots of things I could tell, and you wouldn't like it so much."

"Pooh. I don't care. I don't care about nothing." Gally held out the banana peel in two fingers, let it fall. But before it hit the floor, she caught it with her left hand. Grinning at Shaw, she turned and, twitching her round little buttocks, left the room.

Shaw returned to Vinnie. "I don't like to sound troublesome, Mrs. Bethea, but there's quite a bit at stake. No good citizen has a right to withhold information. So I'll have to ask you again, do you know who Mr. Big is?"

"No, sir, Mr. Lieutenant, I surely don't know. I wouldn't like to know something like that. I just mind my own business, and that way I don't make no trouble."

Shaw laughed. "You've got the wrong idea, Mrs. Bethea. You're a tax-payer, a citizen; the police department is organized to protect you, but you've got to help the police department."

Vinnie mulishly shook her head. "That's what they say." Her voice expressed cynicism and doubt. Gally strolled back into the room, having made use of the interval to fluff out her hair. An engaging young creature, thought Shaw, for all her perverse flippancy. Gally said, "C'mon, Vinnie, don't be that way. Sly old thing. Tell Mr. Fuzz what he wants to know."

Vinnie swung toward Gally lips drawn back from her teeth in embarrassment and rage. "That's about enough of you! I ain't gonna put up with it!"

"Pooh," said Gally, "I'm too old to whip and too mean to scare."

"You ain't too old and mean to be hit with a stick, I know that much."

Gally shook her head in whimsical disapproval toward Shaw. "Ain't she the one though. But don't let her kid you: she—" Gally's voice dwindled and died, as a door scraped open at the back of the house. They heard the thump of heavy footsteps. Vinnie sat utterly still. Gally turned, marched briskly out the front door.

Into the room came a man about fifty years old, limping slightly. His skin was the color of charred wood. He was almost six feet tall, heavy in the shoulders, deep in the chest with long arms, a long waist, legs disproportionately short. His hair was cropped close, his eyes were small, narrow; his nose flat against his face. Bands of muscle surrounded his mouth, his chin was flat and heavy.

Shaw rose to his feet; the two men stood looking at each other. Neither spoke. The newcomer turned, eyed Vinnie, as if making her a silent dire promise. Vinnie sat speechless, twisting her hands. The man turned, limped back into the kitchen. Shaw heard the back door open and shut.

He turned to Vinnie. "Who is that?"

Vinnie said weakly, "Oh—he's just a man what comes around, works on the house. Kinda the landlord."

Shaw hardened his voice. "Let's quit beating around the bush. I'm convinced that you can tell me a lot of what I want to know. You're going to tell me, either here or down at headquarters. If you won't talk, we'll lock you up as a material witness."

"I ain't witness to anything," complained Vinnie Bethea. "You ain't got a right to treat folks so."

"Mrs. Bethea," said Shaw, "I'm not interested if you've been defrauding the Welfare Department. It's a crime and I'm obliged to arrest criminals, but right now I want Mr. Big. If you tell me what you know, I'll forget anything I've seen and heard. If you don't, I'll order a complete investigation. If you've obtained welfare payments by fraud, you'll go to jail and you'll never receive another cent."

Vinnie Bethea held gnarled hands to her face.

"Who is that man?" demanded Shaw. "Your husband?"

"I can't tell you nothing," moaned Vinnie. "He'll treat me bad."

"You'd better tell me everything, or I'll treat you worse. That man is Si Bethea?"

Vinnie nodded. "But he don't give me no money. Not a cent. I give money to him."

"Is he Mr. Big?"

Vinnie looked up in surprise and indignation. "Si? He ain't no such thing. If Si could put his hands on Mr. Big, I feel sorry for that chiselin' man."

"How do you know Si isn't Mr. Big?"

"Because I seen the way he acted."

"The way he acted when?"

Vinnie drew a deep hopeless breath. "Mr. Lieutenant, I just couldn't help it. That man left me; he left me cold. Then I got on Welfare with that free money and he began coming back. If the Welfare stopped, he'd go again. I couldn't know what to do; I prayed to the good Lord to help me."

Shaw held up his hand. "Just tell me what happened."

"All right, I'll tell you, Mr. Lieutenant. Like I say, Si run off someplace down Seventh Street, never told me nothing, not even goodby. But he left the children here, and I got to watch out for them. Ainsworth he's my own child and he ain't so bad, but that Galatea, she's enough to drive a person wild. So persnickety like." She laughed, suddenly malicious. "But I don't care. I ain't gonna help her no more. It says in the Book, 'Forgive them, they know not what they do', but not Gally. She knows just too much what she do. She's what they call a limb of Satan, and that's the truth. With Si in the hospital it got so I couldn't stand it; I took Ainsworth away—"

Shaw interrupted. "What about Mr. Big?"

Vinnie paused. "I don't know much about that Mr. Big business."

"Just tell me what you do know."

"Well, I heard about Mr. Big from some friends at the church, ladies who happen to be on Welfare. I heard them cussin' Mr. Big up and down. I asked about it and they turned all innocent-like. 'Mr. Big? Who's he?' and I said 'I heard you talkin' him down.' They laughed like it was all fun, and I didn't know any different until one morning it must have been three months ago... Maybe four, I don't remember just right... I was at home with the children. Si was working a poker game—that's what he is, Mr. Lieutenant, a no-count poker-playing gambler. I knew he was playing; he took all my money, but he said he'd be back in the morning with a big roll of bills. About nine o'clock it must have been when I heard him coming along the street. Not drunk exactly; mainly he was tired..."

At nine o'clock Si Bethea came along Van Buren Avenue from the direction of Seventh Street, smoking a big cigar. He wore a baggy roan-red suit, a limp white shirt open at the collar. He was unshaven, his eyes were pink with fatigue. He had played poker for eleven straight hours; he had won four dollars. Not counting a fifth of whiskey and five dishes of barbecue. Nothing to crow about, but better than losing. There had been an argument with a shifty arrow-faced longshoreman called Panama Slim. Panama Slim had jumped to his feet, hand in his coat pocket. "You say you put out your ante, where's all the money?" Si had sat staring at Panama Slim, burning him with unutterable promises. He said slowly, "If a man don't like the game, he better find a new place to play."

Panama Slim forced a sudden jocularity upon himself; he settled back into the chair. "Jus' a mistake all round," he said magnanimously. "This is a friendly game; I don't give shucks for a measly two-bit piece. I got lots of 'em."

Si gained face by the episode. Panama Slim was considered a dangerous man.

So coming along Van Buren Avenue, Si's mood was neither exultation nor dejection. He felt pretty mean and cantankerous, but that was the whiskey and long hours under a bare bulb.

Ahead was his house. Welfare paid the rent, Welfare bought the groceries. Let 'em. Big-shot white men wanted to pay his rent, buy his groceries, Si wasn't about to stop it.

He turned into the yard, banged the gate behind him. Now they knew he was coming. When the women-folk took respect of him they hustled and didn't jaw so much. Although he never got blind crazy drunk anymore; seem like the whiskey had lost its bite. He had not been home in four days, except to take a little spare change off of Vinnie. One time she'd been a pretty good woman, the last two three years she'd let herself go.

Vinnie looked out of the window and made an admonitory gesture. Vinnie didn't like any ructions, said if the Welfare Man heard of Si's coming in and out they'd stop the money. "Better not stop that money,"

Si had warned her. "You gettin' pretty long in the tooth to hustle, but that's where you be."

Si proceeded to the back porch, pushed open the door, entered the house.

Vinnie was excited. "You tryin' to throw us all in jail? Slammin' the gate like that! Them nosy people see you come in —"

"Don't give me no jaw. Get some vittles on the stove."

Vinnie cried defiantly, "That Welfare Man's comin' today. Sposin' he comes early. He see you, we get trouble."

"He come in the front door, I go out the back." Si held up his hand. "Don't you worry, I do the worrying 'round here. Get them vittles goin'."

Gally came into the kitchen. "Hey, Pa."

"What you up to?"

"You win?"

"Sure I win."

"I wanta buy something."

Si shook his head. "I need that money. I got a big game goin' tonight. Can't afford no foolishness."

Vinnie muttered under her breath.

"What's that?" Si demanded. "You say something?"

"I said, the Welfare Man's gonna come and catch you here like a toad in a puddle. Then he call the police —"

Footsteps sounded on the front porch. Vinnie held up her hand in an attitude of despair. "That's him now. Oh my Lord, what did I say? You get yourself gone!"

Gally said, "It's the mail man. Relax." She went out into the hall, picked up the letter which had fallen through the slot.

Back in the kitchen, Vinnie was frying eggs.

"What's that?" rumbled Si. "Lemme see that letter."

"It's for Vinnie."

"Don't give me sass. You still ain't too big for whippin'."

Gally became instantly quiet. She dreaded the thought of Si's hands on her. Someday he might catch hold of her, then nothing could help her.

Vinnie came across the kitchen, held out her hand. "Who's it from?"

Si took the letter. Vinnie drew back her hand, went to tend the eggs. Si tore open the envelope, drew out the folded paper. He read it slowly, cigar jiggling as his lips moved. He read it a second time. He put it down, sat thinking.

Dishing up the eggs, Vinnie said in a petulant voice, "Might at least let on who's writin'."

Si made no answer. Vinnie slid the eggs down in front of him. "I ask you, who's writin' me?"

Si said in a heavy voice, "Mr. Big."

Vinnie emitted a peculiar wail. "Oh, that Mr. Big!"

Gally snatched the letter, read it aloud.

> Dear Mrs. Virginia Bethea:
>
> You are CHEATING THE GOVERNMENT. You draw big Welfare money and your husband lives at home. You know that is a CRIME!
>
> I like some of that money. $10 a week. You pay me, everything is okay. You do not pay me, I will give the Welfare Man proof that you are a LIAR and a CHEATER. You will go to JAIL. They will cut off your money. You will be DISGRACED.
>
> Every week, so long as you draw Welfare, put $10 bill into envelope, mail to:
>
> MR. BIGLEY
> BOX 4912
> OAKLAND, CALIFORNIA
>
> Do this without fail.
>
> Do not tell ANYBODY about this letter or how you send money. If you tell you will be in BIG trouble.
>
> Sincerely yours,
> MR. BIG

"Ain't that just awful?" cried Vinnie in a reedy voice.

Si grunted, spread margarine across a piece of bread, started on the eggs.

Vinnie poured herself a cup of coffee, sat down at the table, gazed bleakly into the steam. "I don't know what to do. Ain't enough money now, you gamblin' away every cent. I might as well just throw myself in the bay."

"Pour me some of that coffee."

Vinnie lifted the pot automatically, then turned in indignation. "You hear what I said? Ain't no money and now, just on account of you, this Mr. Big wants ten dollars a week."

Si shook his head. "He ain't gonna get it."

"No? How you gonna stop him? You let him put me in jail?"

"Pour that coffee, woman."

"I pour it over your head. What you gonna do about this?"

"I ain't gonna do nothing."

Vinnie said bitterly, "You don't care if I'm in jail. Except then the money don't come in."

"I take care of this."

"I suppose you know this Mr. Big."

"I know he don't fool with Si Bethea."

Gally said in an airy voice, "The Welfare Man's come to the door."

Vinnie whimpered in anguish, "You get outa here, Si Bethea! Don't you let him see you! Oh Lord have mercy!"

The door bell rang. Si unhurriedly pushed the last of his eggs into his mouth, sauntered out upon the back porch. Vinnie put the dish in the sink, threw the unfinished coffee back into the pot. "Gally, you go answer that door."

Gally strolled to the door, swung it open with an impertinent jerk, exercising her personality in even so staid an act. "Hello, Mr. Welfare Man."

"Oh. Hello there. I haven't seen you before."

"Sometimes I'm in, sometimes I'm out. Today I'm in."

"You must be one of the children."

Gally glanced down along her long legs, shapely in the leopard-spot leotards. "I look like a child?"

"I better not answer that. Can I come in?"

"I guess so. You want to see Vinnie? She's out in the kitchen. I'll call her."

"Don't bother; the kitchen's good enough for me."

Vinnie was nervously sitting at the table drinking coffee. "Oh, excuse me, Mr. Gunther. I didn't quite expect you today. Maybe you like a cup of coffee? Gally, pour out a cup. I forget, Mr. Gunther, do you take cream and sugar?"

"Just black, thanks. How're you getting on?"

"Oh, just barely so-so, Mr. Gunther. Things is so high. I need my refrigerator fixed, it don't get cold or nothing. The children want new clothes, it's hard to get by."

Paul nodded, raised his head, sniffed. Vinnie looked at him in alarm. "What's the matter, Mr. Gunther?"

"Seems like I smell a cigar."

"Cigar?" Vinnie looked wildly around the room, then said, "I like a little smoke once in a while...just now and again. Don't do it much in front of the children..." Her voice drifted away. Gally giggled, Vinnie turned her a wild glare.

Paul pursed his lips. "I see. Where's your husband?"

"That I don't know, Mr. Gunther. Like I told you he just up and took off."

"You haven't seen him?"

"I don't want to see him, Mr. Gunther. I wish that man never crossed my path!"

"No support comes in from him? No funds whatever?"

Vinnie shook her head bitterly. "Nothing at all, Mr. Gunther, and that's a fact."

Paul opened his briefcase, removed a clip-board. "Two children. Galatea, Ainsworth, right?"

"Yes sir."

"How they getting on?"

"Very good, Mr. Gunther. Ainsworth, he's in school. Gally here she's thinking about a secretarial course, something like that."

Paul looked speculatively toward Gally, who was leaning against the wall, filing her nails. "Well, let's see what we can do for you. You say your refrigerator's gone out?"

"Just don't seem to work," Vinnie said mournfully.

"Well, here's what you do. Call a repair man in, see what he says. If he can fix it, tell him to go ahead. Then call me down at the Welfare Department and let me know how much it'll be. I'll try to get you something extra."

"I don't know," said Vinnie. "I think the thing's just plumb busted."

"Stupid old box," said Gally. "It just makes a noise like k-k-k-k-k-k. Then that's all. Just the noise."

"Well, you let me know," said Paul. "You've got to have a refrigerator, no question about that. Maybe I can work something out."

"That would be nice, Mr. Gunther."

"How's everything else? Keeping up on your rent?"

"Just a little behind on the rent, Mr. Gunther."

"How come? I thought we worked out a budget for you."

Vinnie nodded miserably. Si had taken the rent money for his big-time poker game. She'd never see it back. "Well, things come up. Ainsworth caught a cold and I had to buy medicine. There was new shoes, things like that. That money just gets eaten up, Mr. Gunther. I really don't know where it goes."

Paul shook his head dubiously. "I can't get you any more subsistence. I don't know how you're going to make your rent."

"I don't know either, Mr. Gunther."

"Well, you'll have to cut a few dollars a week off your groceries. You do that, in two months you'll be caught up."

"I guess that's what we gotta do," said Vinnie glumly.

"You'd better give the news to your landlord. The sooner he knows the better he'll like it."

"I'll tell him first thing this morning."

"And you'll call me about your refrigerator?"

"Yes, I surely will, Mr. Gunther."

Paul rose to his feet. "Thanks for the coffee. Don't bother," he said as Vinnie started to rise. "I'll find my own way out." Vinnie sank back into her chair. Some days life wasn't worth it.

Gally went to the door with Paul. "You're a hard-hearted man. Make poor Vinnie go without her cigars."

"How about you?" Paul paused on the porch. "You going without anything?"

"I don't smoke cigars. I like other stuff better."

"Such as what?"

Gally slid pliantly up against the door-jamb. "Such as stuff. Just stuff."

Paul laughed. "You're a mighty cute little chick."

"I got what I need. Where you going now?"

"I'm going to lunch. Want to come? You'd better not. I'd eat you up in just one bite."

Gally nuzzled the jamb with her cheek. "I'm pretty tough, and wiggly too."

"You look like you might be. I got to check on that sometime."

From the kitchen came Vinnie's voice. "Gally, what you doing?"

"Talking to the Welfare Man," said Gally over her shoulder. "He's just checking, like he's supposed to do."

Vinnie came to the kitchen door, peered suspiciously down the hall. Paul grinned, encompassing both Vinnie and Gally. "Goodby then. I'll see what I can do about that refrigerator." He ran down the steps, jumped into his car.

"Mmf," sniffed Vinnie. "You be careful of them white boys. Don't pay to truck with them."

"They're just as good as black," said Gally airily. "So they say, anyway."

Vinnie shook her head stubbornly. "Don't pay to mix; it just makes trouble. You let your father catch you, he'll give you real what-for."

"Pooh. He just say one word to me..." Gally shrugged her shoulders impudently. "He ain't one to talk."

Vinnie turned away. She had problems enough without Gally. The rent money, to come out of the groceries. Ten dollars a week to Mr. Big. "Looks like we'll be eatin' mighty poor for a while," she told Gally, drearily.

Gally patted her shoulder. "I don't care. But if I was you I wouldn't give Si another cent."

Vinnie shook her head. "Easier said than done."

Vinnie sat with her hands twisting in her lap. "That's what I know about Mr. Big. I got the letter, I scrimped and cut down, I tried to make up the money. Then Si come and took it."

"He took the money for Mr. Big?"

Vinnie nodded. "He said not to pay Mr. Big. He was going to look him up and talk to him personally."

"Do you know if he did?"

"He wouldn't tell me. I guess he tried. One day he took Ainsworth out on some kind of business. Ainsworth wouldn't say where they went, since his daddy told him to button his lip. They went out — oh, I guess it was the day after the letter came. And that was the end of it because Si got run down by a car. Everybody thought he was dead." Vinnie shook her head in reluctant admiration. "Can't kill that man. He's too mean to kill."

"Who run him down?" asked Shaw.

"We never did find out. One of them hit-runners. Si was drunk. The doctor says that's what saved him. He just got out of the hospital a week ago."

"And what about Mr. Big after that?"

"I got another letter. It said, 'How come you ain't payin' my money? Look sharp or I make it $20 a week.' "

"So you paid?"

Vinnie said sheepishly, "I didn't feel I could not pay. Then just yesterday I got a letter saying not to send any more money."

"Do you still have that letter?"

"I threw it away."

"Mmf... How much of this did you tell Paul Gunther?"

"Nothing. Last Friday he asked what I knew about Mr. Big. I said I never heard of him."

Shaw rose, walked back and forth across the room. In the five households Paul Gunther had visited Friday, no one admitted giving him information. Five down, none to go. He asked Vinnie, "I don't suppose he said where he was going after he left you?"

"No sir. I seen him talking to Gally, and her squirming around like a snake got in her drawers. I went to put a stop to it. Mr. Gunther took off. He went down to the service station and bought gas." Vinnie pointed out the window toward the service station at the corner of Ninth and Van Buren. "I saw him talking to the man there, and after that I don't know what happened. And I sure don't want to know."

"When does Ainsworth get home from school?"

Vinnie looked at him in puzzled protest. "What in the world do you want with Ainsworth?"

"I want to ask him a few questions. What time will he be here?"

"Along about three-thirty. Unless he stops to fool along the way."

Shaw thought a moment. "I'll be back at four o'clock. In the meantime don't talk to Ainsworth about me. Don't even tell him I want to see him. Do you understand?"

"Whatever you say, Mr. Lieutenant."

Chapter VII

Ted Therbow

Shaw walked pensively back to his car. Si Bethea, like Paul Gunther, had gone out to find Mr. Big. Paul Gunther was dead, Si Bethea had spent three months in the hospital. Shaw frowned in perplexity. Was Mr. Big's identity so sensitive, so vulnerable, that he felt he had to kill to protect it?

Shaw stopped short, looked back at the old house on the corner. It told him nothing. The maddening questions remained: How? Why?

Shaw made a sound in his throat, turned and continued to his car. Another thought obtruded into his mind: of the five clients Paul had interviewed Friday, none admitted giving him information. Had Paul consulted someone else? Shaw appraised the service station across the street, where, according to Vinnie, Paul had stopped after leaving her house.

Shaw crossed the street. The attendant, a stocky negro in faded suntans, the name 'Nick' embroidered on his shirt, watched him approach. Shaw displayed his badge; Nick growled, "What is it this time?"

"I want some information," said Shaw.

"I got some good street maps," said Nick. "You don't need the badge to pick up a map."

"I don't want a map," said Shaw. "I'm interested in last Friday."

Nick examined Shaw with cynical interest. "You working on that killing up the street?"

"That's right. Were you on duty last Friday?"

"I'm here all day every day."

"About two o'clock a man in a green Mercury sedan drove in. Do you remember seeing him?"

"What year Mercury?"

"That's something I don't know. I'd guess about two or three years old."

"Black man?"

"No, white. About twenty-five years old, dark-haired; nice-looking fellow."

Nick shook his head. "I don't remember him. You might ask Ted there under the rack. He was working Friday."

Shaw went into the lubrication shed. A tall young black in white coveralls stood beneath a lavender and white Cadillac hardtop. As Shaw approached he removed the plug from the pan and a dark golden column sprang instantaneously down into the heart of the waiting funnel.

"Yes, sir," said Ted, waiting for the oil to drain. "What can I do for you?"

Shaw identified himself, asked his questions. Ted looked at him sidelong, not answering for a moment. Shaw waited.

"Yes," said Ted, after a pause of five seconds. "I saw that man. If you're talking about Paul Gunther, and I guess you are."

This was better than Shaw had hoped. "You know him?"

"Not real intimate-like. I've seen him at parties."

"You've heard he's dead, of course."

Ted nodded. "I read about it in the papers. Happened in that old house just down the street." The shiny column of oil collapsed into a flutter of heavy drops. Ted Therbow replaced the plug, then, emerging from under the car, wiped his hands on a rag.

Shaw had been studying him with a frowning intensity. "Do you know anything about the killing?"

Ted laughed uneasily. "Come now, Lieutenant. Things that simple just don't happen, do they?"

"No," said Shaw, "I'm afraid not. We've got to do everything the hard way. But maybe you can tell me something, some little fact, to give me a line on the killer. Or even on why Gunther was killed."

Ted Therbow shook his head. "I haven't any idea, Lieutenant. The thing came as a big surprise to me."

"What did he talk about when he was in here Friday?"

Ted frowned. "Didn't seem like it was much. 'How you been doing?' 'Know a good bash for tonight?' That kind of thing."

"And that's the last you saw of him?"

"That's the last."

"You've no idea why anyone should want to kill him?"

Ted shrugged. "I suppose there's people who didn't like Paul, just like there's people who don't like me and don't like you. I don't think any of them cut his throat."

"Who are these people?"

Ted shook his head. "Don't pin me down there, Lieutenant. I just couldn't say."

"And wouldn't if you could, eh?"

Ted grinned. "I wouldn't want to put the finger on anybody unless I knew something for sure."

"Do you know where Gunther lived?"

"No, guess I don't," said Ted after reflection. "I've sold him gas from time to time. Come to think, he usually drove in from Ninth, if that's any help to you."

"Did you ever hear him mention Mr. Big?"

"Nope...Wait. Yes he did. First time I ever met him, at a party in Berkeley. We got talking about West Oakland, and the crooks down here. I guess you know there's lots of them. Mr. Big came up somehow. Nothing much was said, not that I recall." Ted pursed his lips in an expression of melancholy humor. "Talk about trouble, that party made lots of trouble for Paul."

"How so?"

Ted hesitated, then shrugged. He said in a subdued voice, "Well, here's where Paul met this Barbara chick. I guess he played her a real pretty tune, because about a month later I saw them at another party, really look like both of 'em had it bad. Couldn't take their eyes off each other. Well, that was nice. But Paul is real strange. He's got a heart full of love for most any sweet young gal." Ted shook his head wryly. "I'll tell you how it happened, if you're interested."

"Oh yes," said Shaw. "I'm interested. Highly interested."

Ted looked out toward the front of the station. Nick stood by the gas-pump watching him. Ted picked up the grease-gun and began shooting grease into the front-end fittings. "Well, like I say, I know this beat-type character Cat Catson, lives down here in West Oakland. Days he works in the cannery, nights he blossoms like a beautiful flower. Plays the bongos, paints pictures, just plain generates atmosphere. And not a bad guy at all; in fact he's a damn fine fellow. Do anything for anybody. A while back Cat stages this party. Jam-session kind of party; you know, musicians and such. I noodle around on the flute, so I always shape up when Catson sends out the invitation. I arrived about nine, which is early, but I like to sit quiet and watch things develop.

"About ten o'clock who comes in but Paul with a real sweet lil black chick. I was surprised, because last time I saw Paul he was gone on this pretty Barbara ..."

Gally came to the party in a new cocoa suit which had cost something under thirty dollars at J.C. Penney's. Nobody need know that, of course. She and Paul sat close together on a very low couch, Gally quivering, jerking her knees with happy excitement. Cat (the Cat) Catson and his flat were new experiences for her; she knew such people existed, of course, but she never had mingled with them.

Gally studied the walls, which originally had been white plaster. Now, wherever she looked, artists had painted pictures directly on the walls! Pictures everywhere! Abstract compositions, surrealist landscapes, nudes of every description, snow-flake designs and milk-weed fluff, dragons and monsters, unclassifiable blotches, daubs, and smears. Fascinating! thought Gally. Fun! She squeezed Paul's hand. "How I wish I could learn to be an artist! I love these things!" She waved her hand around the room, indicating both the paintings, and Catson's other knickknacks, books, fetishes, totems, symbols, jugs, bottles, metal-work, masks, ashtrays and figures.

Paul forbore the sententious pronouncement that Gally had fallen in love, not with art, but with the atmosphere. Gally was young; it would be a shame to stifle her enthusiasm.

In the room were about a dozen people. Cat Catson, a diffident young man with aquiline delicate features, skin the color of mocha ice cream, was arranging his bongos. Ted Therbow stood in the corner, blowing soft muttery whispers from his flute. A short heavy-shouldered white lad with a beard like dry tumbleweed sat at the piano, rippling idle arpeggios. Beside him stood Egon Briar, a thin white man of thirty, with unkempt black hair, a pinched jaw, burning black eyes under barred black eyebrows. He wore brown slacks, a black shirt, and clutched a notebook in hands tense as talons. He professed to be a poet, and Paul suspected the name Egon Briar to be a pseudonym.

Counting Gally, there were five girls in the room, three white and two black. One of the white girls had brought a guitar, but no one suggested that she play. Perhaps later.

The door opened, two more men and a girl came in, bringing a string bass, a tenor saxophone. Catson called out: "Where's Peynton?"

"Can't make it," said one of the newcomers.

"Goddam," muttered Catson. "I wanted that horn bad."

"Oh, we got better than Peynton. Do you know Chang Onsberger?"

"With the flugel? He here?"

"Just parking."

"Great. Simply great."

The door opened; in came a gush of people led by a vast young white man with a flugelhorn. There were six in his entourage: two white girls, and four men, two black.

"Howdy all," said Chang. "What are we blowing?"

"Nothing yet," said Catson seriously. "Glad you showed."

"Thanks." Chang looked sidelong toward Egon Briar. "That the canary? I never worked this kind of gig before."

"Briar wanted to try it," said Catson. "He's pretty well known; it might work out."

Chang brought out his flugelhorn, blew scales. The string bass got A from the piano, tuned. The tenor sax adjusted his reed.

Paul took Gally's glass, went out in the kitchen, came back with refills of red wine. Gally looked up at him, eyes shining, arms clasped around her knees.

"I gotta learn to play something," said Gally with decision. "I always wanted piano lessons, but Si wouldn't allow it. Said musicians were all bums."

Paul asked whimsically, "What would he say if he knew about us?"

Gally shrugged. "Nothing much." This was a statement which neither believed.

"We won't tell him," said Paul.

"Were we gonna tell anybody?"

Paul frowned. Gally's humor occasionally was biting.

More people came into the room. From somewhere Paul caught the smell of grass, but looking around could not detect the source.

Gally caught the odor. She nudged Paul. "Somebody's blowing some grass."

"You ever smoke?" asked Paul.

"Sure," said Gally. "Now and then."

The B-flat blues dwindled and died, the musicians looked around at each other in satisfaction. Egon Briar, leaning on the piano, came over to Catson, spoke a few words. Catson nodded. Briar turned to the other musicians, cleared his throat. The musicians watched him with wary curiosity. "I wrote these pieces especially for recitation to music," said Briar. "Since this is the first time you've heard them, I'll read each twice. First time you can play if you like, but mainly you should concentrate on the mood of the poem."

"What key?" asked Chang.

Briar shrugged petulantly. "That's your problem. Whatever you like." He opened his notebook. "This first is a little impression after the manner of the Japanese haiku. It has no name, but merely presents a scene, a mood. I'll read it."

Black curl of spume, half surround the gray stone
Wide and white comes the dawn down low
And smash
Sparkle teeth
The corescent yellow hammer
The world must spin again.

"Is that all?" asked Chang.

Egon Briar nodded. "Just a sensation, an experience."

"Quite Jungian," said the tenor sax.

"Precisely," said Egon Briar.

"It doesn't give us much scope for a melodic line," said Chang.

"Certainly it does." Egon Briar reached. "May I blow your bugle?"

Chang passed it over. With impressive gravity Egon Briar propped the notebook on a chair, studying the poem as if it were a musical score. He blew a blast from the flugelhorn, then with astonishing facility, created a snatch of mysterious tune. The tenor sax blew, the piano started the chords, the bongos, string-bass, flute set out in full cry.

Egon Briar finished, the tenor sax honked a second verse. Primly Egon Briar raised the flugelhorn, blew a sustaining note. The solo went to Ted; Egon Briar and the tenor sax playing a soft riff. Chang began snapping his fingers.

The piano soloed. Egon Briar raised the horn. "Here," called Chang. "You cats trying to stomp off and leave old Chang with his pants down. Gimme my horn, you pirate."

The music stopped, except for the string bass and the bongos, still pounding out rhythm.

"Well," said Egon Briar, "that's how it goes."

"I see," said Chang. "Yes sir, I think I can make it."

The poem was read; the music was played, rather more sedately than before.

There was applause.

"Now," said Briar, "another short mood." He addressed the audience, half-defensively. "You understand I am purposely avoiding social comment. This is a flow of image and mood and melody. I leave polemic to the geologists."

Gally whispered to Paul, "The what to the which?"

"Polemic is argument. Geologists I don't know...Unless he means Republicans."

"Oh."

Egon Briar turned the page of his notebook. "I call this 'Background'."

He read:

Wail in the forest
Shudder and thump
By far trail to north and east

Through realm of Scyth and Cimmerian
Through time of surprise, the making of laws
Each tree a tall god
Walk with fear, they chop and hack
They hunt
They kill without fail
These murdering tribal brothers.

He looked at the musicians. "No flute on this, no piano, no bass. Just the drums and horn and tenor. The sound should be gruff, hoarse, yet smooth and slow. Got it?"

"E-flat," Chang told the tenor. "You lead, I'll play harmony."

Egon Briar re-read the poem:

"Background:"

Wail in the forest—

Gally listened. "That's a scary one. Gives me spooks, all that killing."

Paul drank his wine. "How you doing?"

"I got enough for now."

Egon Briar held up his hand authoritatively. "This next one is longer. It concerns itself with the ever-lengthening perspectives of age, and it's called 'When You and I Were Why Mac'."

He read, rather slowly:

Red as new blood
White as milk
Black as midnight
Green as next door's lawn
Green as looking-up the sun through leaves
Green as focused water.

Yellow as sunflower, sand
Yellow as butter, with chicken-fat and mustard
On yellow cake, egg-yolks for candles
Yellow as yellowest yellow, cheese and beach-towels.

Brown as scurvy
Brown as farmer's dirt
Brown as you-know-what
Brown as new shoes, with henna and snuff and a fare-thee-well
Brown as drunken Rembrandt.
Then: majesty.
The attributes of all things are known by their glory.
The orange orange, the blue of ink and marble,
the purple pajamas
Rich as handfuls of melted crayon.

Now with webs and rickets and eye-glass dim:
Supercilious vista: tweeds and rain and whole-wheat bread
A clean shirt for the morning.
No more magic, but we are wise, and all know where we die.

The second version, the music. Paul said under his breath, "Oh Lord."

Gally pressed close to him. "What's the matter?"

"Nothing," said Paul. There was a faint prickle of sweat on his forehead. He glanced from the corner of his eye toward the two late-comers: Jim Connor the astronomer, and Barbara Tavistock.

Barbara nodded to Paul, a twitch at the corners of her mouth. Connor apparently had never seen Paul before.

Paul thought, I love her. Do I? He turned his eyes to the musicians, feeling Gally's thigh taut against his own. I don't love Gally. But I do — as I might love a kitten. What a condescending son-of-a-bitch I am. What a plain ordinary son-of-a-bitch. Still — I don't care too much. Life is a serious business. Devil take the hindmost. Let's have some composure. Remember Article 2…

Paul relaxed. The Creed. Nothing could hurt him, nothing could touch him. Anything was easy, so long as he kept the Creed to the front of his mind.

Of course, there was Jim Connor. Jim Connor, unpredictable, protean, unique. How could Destiny, even Destiny, have contrived such a special example? Jim Connor's apparent — that was the word *apparent* — individualism sometimes seemed more intense than Paul's own. It must be disproved.

Egon Briar finished his poem; the musicians continued playing, entranced with the momentum of their music. Egon Briar smiled rather foolishly at the crowd, made a nondescript gesture, went to lean on the piano.

The musicians, bored with the poetry, played. Egon Briar went into the kitchen, where he drank several glasses of wine.

Barbara and Jim crossed the room to stand in frônt of Paul and Gally. This was at Barbara's initiative. Jim Connor's face showed a glimmer of uninterested recognition as he looked down at Paul. Barbara smiled brightly, "I had no idea I'd see you here, Paul."

"I'm liable to turn up anywhere. Have a seat. Miss Bethea — Miss Tavistock, Mr. Connor. Gally, Barbara, Jim."

"Hi." "How do you do?"

"You've missed the poetry," said Paul. "But don't go away. Egon Briar is in the kitchen composing an ode."

"We heard a little of it as we came in," said Barbara. "Did you like it?"

"Oh..." Paul shrugged. "It was interesting. They proved nothing very much."

"How could they?" Jim Connor demanded contemptuously. "The idea's a farce to begin with."

Paul considered. He entered arguments only when he knew he could win them. Always, before committing himself, he made a careful mental reconnaissance. In this case he could see a clear and cogent continuity of ideas. He decided to argue. He would force Jim Connor to back away, to acknowledge him powerful, distinct, singular... Paul said slowly, "Given one or two conditions — intelligent musicians, intelligible poetry — the two pursuits aren't incommensurable."

Jim said disinterestedly, "You're a humanist. Humanism, subjectivism, sentimentality — whatever it's called — is an opiate. It vitiates your judgment."

Paul said lightly, "The subject demands a humanist approach. How can we intelligently discuss these people except on their own terms?"

Connor nodded. "A good point. I stand corrected. No doubt I'm prejudiced." He looked around the room with distaste. "What a clutter. Disorganization."

Gally squirmed and said in an eager voice, "I like this pad. It's all bright and happy. Don't you feel it? Come along now, you're not so old-fashioned as all that. Live a little! Drink some of that wine! Relax!"

Connor laughed. "Oh, the enthusiasm of youth."

"So I'm young," Gally admitted. "But I'm a swingin' woman. I like different things. I like these happy cats."

"That's all very good," said Connor. "But you shouldn't confuse novelty with originality, feverish activity with gayety."

"Man, you're square." Gally leaned forward, inspected Jim. "Where do you live?"

"Thirteen-twenty La Honda Road."

"What's your pad like? You got pictures on the walls? Books? Any of these little dangling things?"

"You're asking me what kind of facade I put up? Gally, here's the truth. I'm a spotted lizard. I take the color of my surroundings. I don't like to be noticed."

"But you didn't answer my question."

Connor waved his hand in a gesture of unconcern. "So I have a few books. I keep them in a book-case, which is painted white. The books are about mathematics, astronomy, cybernetics. There are about two hundred pictures on the wall. The walls are painted white. The pictures are black line drawings, on a white background. They have titles like $xy^3 + \sqrt{xy} = 3$."

"Oh?" said Barbara. "That sounds interesting. What are these pictures?"

"Graphs of equations. I collect them. $x^2 + y^2 = 9$. That's a circle with a radius of three units. You probably know that. The other curves are more complex. Some are surprising. They're all beautiful." He glanced toward Paul. "Not at all subjectivist."

"Have you resigned from the human race?" asked Paul, and immediately thought fretfully, why am I saying this? He should be saying that to me!

"I'm resigned to the human race. I can't help being human."

"Man," said Gally, with great feeling, "You're so square you're sharp on the edges. Isn't he, Paul?"

"Yes," said Paul. "Very square."

Connor laughed with what Paul considered hateful complacence. "I'm accustomed to being thought odd."

"Don't be so proud of yourself," Barbara said indulgently. "Not while you're with ordinary mortals."

Paul snorted.

The music halted; the musicians refreshed themselves. Ted crossed the room, flute tucked under his arm. He nodded to Paul, sat down beside Gally. "Like the music?"

Gally screwed up her face. "Great. But," she said softly, "it just don't swing."

"No? I thought we were swingin'." He reached out, ruffled her hair. "What you want, you silly chick? Rock-and-roll?"

"I like whatever you got to give me, daddy."

"Here! You get me in trouble. Big trouble."

Jim Connor leaned forward. "May I see your flute?"

"Sure thing." Ted passed it over.

Jim Connor examined it carefully, hefted it. He spoke in a kind of wonder. "I've just learned something. There's nothing human beings make so beautiful as musical instruments! Look at this wonderful little thing. Look at that guitar. And that horn."

Ted took back his flute with quiet satisfaction. "I like 'em all. Music's a big part of life."

Paul leaned back, the nape of his neck against the cushion. He stared at the ceiling. Ted and Jim talked, with Gally inserting arch badinage, maintaining a continual nervous movement: twisting her hands back to back, pressing her knees together, spreading her feet, cocking her head to the side, raising one shoulder, then the other. Barbara sat quietly, listening, watching.

Paul felt stupid and sluggish. Jim Connor was a charlatan, a poser. But how people could be taken in! He was certainly nothing to look at. His face was pinched and immature, his hair stood on end. He showed no taste in clothes; tonight he wore a limp nutmeg-colored sport-coat, gray twill slacks, scuffed black loafers. With his hollow chest and skinny arms he looked like a wet sparrow. No doubt he aroused the maternal instinct in women... Paul frowned. It surprised him that he had not thought to wonder before. What was he doing out with Barbara? Barbara had never mentioned liking or even knowing Jim Connor. Paul turned to find Barbara watching him with her look of brooding speculation. Paul wavered between a sheepish grin and a glance of indignant accusation, and produced what he felt must be only a foolish grimace. Angrily he lurched back against the wall. Barbara's matter-of-fact attitude was almost insulting. Paul took a deep breath. Relax, boy. Use the old psychology. Show her the suave cool-headed Paul Gunther. He leaned forward once more, an airy smile on his lips.

Barbara, meeting his glance, gave a slight slow shake of her head. "Sometimes it's best just to let things settle by themselves, Paul."

"What do you mean?"

"Don't try to explain things. It's too much trouble. Words don't mean anything anyway."

Paul's smile persisted, though his face muscles felt strained and tight. Easy, boy, he told himself. Cool easy-going Paul Gunther. Think. Somehow he'd salvage the situation. Did he want to salvage it? Yes. No. Yes. He rose to his feet. In his most nonchalant voice he said, "Actions speak louder than explanations... Excuse me." Rather pleased with himself he took Gally's empty glass, sauntered out to the kitchen.

Egon Briar sat straddling a chair backwards, talking in a sulky undertone to Cat Catson. A pretty blonde girl leaned back against the table. Bewitching creature, thought Paul, calm and happy as a summer day. She looked around as Paul filled the glasses. Her face was clear and confident: dimples deepened beside her mouth as she noted Paul's interest. Then she looked away... Paul drew a mournful breath, gazed tragically at the sunny flow of hair. This girl had a soul. Barbara was — Barbara. Brooding and intense. Either melancholy or jittering with an incomprehensible excitement. Vitality, yes; passion, no. Never had she given herself to Paul with the poetic ardor he wanted and needed. Paul sighed. Now he wanted to remain in the kitchen, he wanted to talk to this blonde girl. But he turned swiftly and went back into the living room.

Gally sat on the couch with Ted. Barbara and Jim Connor were nowhere to be seen.

Barbara had gone.

Paul's throat felt thick and icy. He joined Gally, handed her a glass of wine. She feigned a shudder of apprehension. "Much more of this stuff, I'll be turning red."

"After that, I don't know," Ted told George Shaw. He shook his head wistfully. "Poor Paul, he looked sick. Because that Barbara is a real sweet chick. You know her?"

"I've talked to her," said Shaw. He'd talked to her, she'd talked to him. But she hadn't mentioned Gally or Cat Catson's party. What else had she held back?

"In a way it was funny," said Ted. "When Barbara came in with this Connor character, I took a look at Paul. I thought, here's a boy caught with his thumbs in the jam-jar. I was right. Barbara really rubbed it in, and in a real cool way. She just pretended nothing had happened. But she was mad. I saw her looking over the lil gal Paul had come in with, and she was asking herself, 'What's she got I haven't got?' "

"Do you know the other girl's name?"

"Gally, that's what they called her. I don't know her last name, but I've seen her around the neighborhood."

Shaw nodded. "Thanks for your help. If you think of anything else, will you give me a call? Lieutenant George Shaw."

"I'll certainly do that, Lieutenant."

By now Ainsworth should be home from school. Shaw walked back to the Bethea house. There was also Gally to talk to, because if Barbara Tavistock had been withholding information, the same applied to Gally.

Shaw pushed open the creaky iron gate, entered the Bethea yard. He climbed the creaking steps, crossed the porch, rang the bell. The door opened, Vinnie's anxious face appeared.

"I'm back again, Mrs. Bethea," said Shaw. "Is Ainsworth home yet?"

"Yes, he's been home several minutes."

"You didn't mention I wanted to talk to him?"

"No sir, I did not." Vinnie resignedly stepped back from the door. "You want to come in, I guess. I'll call Ainsworth."

"I'd like to see him alone, please. And before I go I want to talk to Gally."

"Gally ain't here. She took off."

"Where'd she go?"

Vinnie's voice was tired and cantankerous. "That I can't say. I give up on her. She's old enough to look out for herself now. Any trouble she gets in that's her doing, not mine."

Shaw said, "I'll talk to Ainsworth."

CHAPTER VIII

Ainsworth

AINSWORTH BETHEA WAS a gangling furtive lad of twelve or thirteen. His hair was cropped so short that the scalp shone brown between flocculations of bristle. His eyes were large and close to the outer edge of his thin face; like a rabbit, he seemed able to see to the rear. He wore fairly clean gray corduroy trousers, a limp white T-shirt, a belt decorated with red glass jewels. He sidled into the living room, hands in pockets, eyes everywhere but toward Shaw.

Vinnie lurked indecisively in the doorway. Shaw said with a polite smile, "It might be easier, Mrs. Bethea, if Ainsworth and I had a man-to-man talk in private."

Vinnie muttered in disapproval, and went down the hall toward the kitchen.

Shaw said in a comradely voice, "Well, Ainsworth, I understand you want to help me catch one of the local bad men."

Ainsworth licked his lips, looked to the right and left.

"Why not sit down?" suggested Shaw. "Where do you go to school?"

"Down the street a ways."

"What grade are you in?"

"High seventh."

"Do you like school?"

Ainsworth gave his shoulders an indifferent twist. "I like it, I guess."

"You remember Paul Gunther, the Welfare Man?"

Ainsworth scratched his nose, darted Shaw a wary look.

"He was killed. But you probably know that."

Ainsworth nodded with unctuous relish. "Yeah, got hisself stuck."

Shaw said confidentially, "I'll tell you something that's an official secret. He was looking for Mr. Big. We think that Mr. Big killed him."

Ainsworth's face showed fleeting phases of cynicism, doubt, boredom. "I guess maybe it might be."

"I suppose you've heard of Mr. Big?"

"Yeah, I guess."

"Do you know who he is? Have you ever seen him?"

Ainsworth's face was blank. "No sir."

"But after your father got a letter from Mr. Big, you and he went out on some kind of errand. What did you do?"

Ainsworth shuffled his feet uneasily. "Oh, just looked around."

Shaw said patiently, "Let's have it, Ainsworth. The truth."

Ainsworth sat staring at his shoes.

Shaw prompted him. "You and your father left here sometime in the morning. Where did you go?"

"The post office."

"The branch office?"

"No."

"The main office?"

"Yeah."

"What did you do there?"

"We just go in. Look around."

"Look around at what?"

"I don't quite remember. That was a long time ago."

"Not as long as all that. Just last April."

"It was March."

Shaw nodded approvingly. "I knew you had a good memory. So you went to the post office. What did you do then?"

Ainsworth replied. Shaw asked another question, and fragment by fragment extracted Ainsworth's story. Ainsworth presently began to make a game of the interview, responding in a manner which conveyed the minimum information without departing from the truth.

Shaw maintained his patience with difficulty; Ainsworth noted this with complacent amusement, and before Shaw felt that he had wrung Ainsworth dry, his voice was trembling with the effort to maintain calm. And in the shadowed hall behind the door, Vinnie stood like a ghost, listening with curiosity as avid as Shaw's own.

Si summoned Ainsworth from the house with a glare back toward the kitchen where Vinnie called in a voice shrill with anger.

Disdaining reply, Si marched down the street to his car, a black bulge-fendered Buick sedan ten years old. He opened the door, motioned to Ainsworth. "Get in boy; we goin' places."

Without enthusiasm Ainsworth got into the car, watched while Si settled himself behind the driver's seat. "Where we goin', Pa?" he asked.

"We goin' where I'm takin' us." Si pushed the starter button. The motor caught hold with a roar and a blast of smoke. Si shifted, the Buick lurched away from the curb. At the corner of Ninth and Van Buren Si turned left toward the center of town. He drove in portentous silence, except for exclamations of wrath when pedestrians or another automobile challenged his right of way. As they crossed Broadway Si spoke in a voice heavy and rough, but which Ainsworth, with his carefully tuned ear, decided was not threatening, "You listen to me now. I don't want no talk about what we doin' today. Nobody's business. You catch on?"

"Okay, Pa," said Ainsworth.

Si took a cigar from his pocket, stripped away the cellophane with his teeth, bit off the end, spat it out the window. He pushed in the cigar-lighter. "What I mean, I don't want none of these blabber-mouth women knowin' what I do. You keep your tongue quiet, hear?"

"I ain't talkin' to nobody," Ainsworth declared bravely.

"Right. That's just right." The lighter popped out. Si pressed the glowing end to his cigar, blew clouds of smoke from both corners of his mouth. "You do like I say and don't ask no questions. Things work out right, maybe I give you a buck or two."

"What we gonna do, Pa?"

"Ain't I just told you, don't ask no questions? When I say something I mean something. I'm big cheese around here, not you."

Ainsworth nodded mournfully.

"You want to amount to something, you gotta learn to take orders," said Si. "Nowadays that's what counts. Johnny-on-the-spot; he take the cake. Don't let these fool women tell you no different. Gotta handle them women. That's what they like. They respect you then. You go around sneakin' and whinin', you don't get nowhere. Nobody got any use for you." Si disdainfully inspected the cigar, pushed it back into his mouth. "No sir!"

"I guess you right, Pa," said Ainsworth.

"Course I'm right."

They approached the main post office. Si pulled over to the curb, parked. "Come along now."

"Where we goin', Pa?"

"Where you think? Ain't you got no sense?"

Ainsworth blinked thoughtfully. Si got out of the car. "C'mon, boy, hustle."

He set off down the street toward the post office. Ainsworth called after him, "Hey Pa! You ain't paid the parking meter!"

Si made a resonant sound of contempt. "No cop gonna tag *my* car."

But he paused and turned back. "I fix that meter for sure. Don't like them no-good things." He brought out his change, found several pennies. "You watch close, I show you how to do it." He inserted a penny, and without turning the handle, forced another penny into the slot. Now he gave the handle a savage yank. The pointer lurched, halted. Si laid a heavy benevolent hand on the meter. "That meter is fixed, boy. I mean is fixed!"

Ainsworth stared at the meter in wonder. "You do it like that, hey, Pa?"

"That's how I do it, boy."

Si stumped off down the street, Ainsworth running behind like a coach-dog.

They came to the post office, climbed the granite steps, pushed through the heavy doors. Ainsworth looked from side to side, the whites of his eyes showing. The long hall smelled strong of authority and power. Si waved his hand with a proprietary air. "This here's the post office," he told Ainsworth. "You want stamps, you go talk to the stamp man. You want to send money, you go see the money-sendin' man. You got any kind of business connected with the post office, you come here, fix it up. A man got to know these things."

"Sure a big place," said Ainsworth.

Si nodded curtly. "Come along now." Si led the way to the section given over to private boxes. He looked keenly around the entire area, then approached the bronze and glass facade, inspected the individual doors. Under his breath he muttered, "4912...4912...Hey now. Looka there."

Ainsworth peered through the glass panel. A number of letters nested in Box 4912. "All for Mr. Big," said Si huskily. "You see them letters? They got money in 'em. From cheatin' women to Mr. Big. You know something, Ainsworth? We gonna nab onto that Mr. Big."

Ainsworth asked apprehensively, "How we gonna do that, Pa?"

"Look at that box. See it?"

"Yeah, I see it."

"Look at it good. I want you to really look at that box. 'Cause if you make a mistake, you might not like what I do."

Ainsworth studied the box carefully.

"You got it?" demanded Si.

"Yeah, I got it."

"All right. Come over here." He took Ainsworth to a desk beside the wall. "You stand here. Like that. I don't care what you do. Draw pictures. Write out your schoolwork. But don't you never do nothing but watch when a man comes in here. Because pretty soon a man will come in who's Mr. Big. We want to talk to that man. You get me?"

Ainsworth nodded unhappily. "How long do I stay here?"

"Till Mr. Big comes for his mail."

"I gotta go to school."

"Never mind about school. You do what I tell you. I take care of the school."

Ainsworth looked wildly back and forth, but without hope. "What I do when Mr. Big comes in?"

"You go with him. I'll be outside on the steps. Ain't just you that's gotta wait. It's *me*! Every day, from eight o'clock till time they close up."

"They throw me outa here, Pa."

"Nobody gonna bother you," declared Si. "Just me, if the man gets them letters and you don't see him. I bother you good. I bother a blister on your bottom size of a pancake. Get me?"

Ainsworth gave a feeble assent.

"When the man comes, don't you give no sudden jump," said Si. "Don't holler, don't go makin' signs. When he goes out you walk slow and easy after him. I'm out on the steps. You give me the sign. Understand?"

"Yeah."

"Okay, you stand here. You see the box?"

"Yeah. Two from the bottom."

"Don't you let that box outa your sight. Hear me now, Ainsworth?"

"Yeah."

"I'm going out on the steps. Don't forget what I told you."

Si departed and Ainsworth took up his vigil.

He watched the whole of the day. Mr. Big did not come to claim his mail. When the post office closed Si took Ainsworth to a hamburger stand, bought him two hamburgers and a milkshake.

At eight-thirty the next morning Ainsworth and Si were among the first to enter. Si assured himself that the letters still occupied the box, then retired to the steps.

Ainsworth stood restlessly by the desk. His legs began to ache. He moved from one foot to another. He had to go to the toilet. During a moment when there was no one in the section, he ran to the entrance, signaled Si. Si came forward. "What's the matter? The man come?"

"I gotta go to the toilet."

"Okay," said Si magnanimously. "Go ahead. I watch for awhile. You come right back."

The day passed. People came in, inserted keys, twisted knobs, took their mail. Nobody approached Box 4912.

Another day passed. New letters were thrust into the box. Si said in a dark voice, "He better come pretty soon; letters be fallin' back out on the floor."

Ainsworth said grouchily, "He ain't comin'. He knows we're standin' around."

"Bah," said Si. "You think I ain't got this man figgered? You don't know me, boy. This Mr. Big he's bad. Me. I'm *really* bad. Nobody fools with me. I give 'em what they come to get."

Ainsworth took up his post once more. He was beginning to recognize the daily pattern: a rush of early mail-gatherers, a slack till noon when there was another run on the boxes, a slow steady trickle till about four, a final burst of business until fifteen minutes before closing time. He had exhausted the possibilities for entertainment at the desk. Now he slouched, lost in boredom, eyes rolling vacuously from floor to ceiling, aware of comings and goings at the boxes more by intuition than observation. He nearly missed the man who finally came to clean out Box 4912.

The time was four-thirty: rush hour for the boxes. People came continuously to the segmented brass and glass panel, inserted keys, swung open doors. Then the scoop of letters, slam of door, departure.

An old negro limped into view. Ainsworth, bored and dull, paid him no heed. This wasn't Mr. Big. Mr. Big was mean and tough like Pa. Or maybe one of the dangerous young men Ainsworth saw swaggering along Seventh Street.

Lack-lusterly Ainsworth watched the old man, then looked at the floor. He wished he were home in bed. This was tiresome... Some inner sense caused him to look up sharply. The old man was slamming the door to Box 4912. He held the letters in his hands. Ainsworth's heart pounded with excitement. Mr. Big! This old coot? Strange, mighty strange! But there it was!

He was crossing the floor, he was coming toward Ainsworth. Did he know? Did he suspect?

Ainsworth slunk back against the wall.

In a tired voice the old man said, "'Scuse me, sonny. I like to use this desk a minute."

"Yeah." Ainsworth moved away.

The old man leafed through the letters, selected a tan envelope, which he opened. He withdrew a folded manila envelope and a ten dollar bill. He pocketed the ten-dollar bill, opened the envelope. Ainsworth glimpsed a printed address, stamps.

The old man inserted the letters, sealed the flap, went to a letter-drop. With a pang Ainsworth saw the letters disappear.

The old man went to the main entrance. Ainsworth followed, hopping with excitement.

And after Ainsworth, casual-seeming but narrow-eyed with suspicion, came Mr. Big himself. He carried a manila envelope which he had taken from another box.

The old man slowly descended the steps. Ainsworth ran over to Si. "That's him. Right there!"

"Which one? That ol' man?"

From the top of the steps Mr. Big studied the situation.

"Yeah!" exclaimed Ainsworth. "He opened a letter, he took out ten bucks and another envelope. Then he mailed all those letters, right back into the post office!"

"Hmmf," muttered Si. "He don't look like no Mr. Big."

This was true. Mr. Big, watching from an inconspicuous vantage-point, resembled the old negro not at all.

Si started after the old man. Ainsworth ran behind.

Mr. Big followed casually.

Si overtook the old man, tapped him on the shoulder. "Hey, ol' timer. I like to talk to you a minute."

The old man turned his head, inspected Si with dignity. "What you want, mister?"

"Like I say, just a little talk."

"Well, I don't wanta talk. Now you let me be."

"Mr. Ol' Man," growled Si, "I think you better use your head. We just talk a little bit; I ain't gonna hurt you none."

"You right," declared the old man. "You ain't gonna hurt me. Because I'm gonna call the policemen!"

"Go ahead," said Si contemptuously. "You know who gets in trouble? You. I see you doin' something that looks pretty guilty. You ever hear of usin' the mails to defraud? That's just what you up to now."

"I don' defraud nobody," roared the old man.

"Maybe you do, maybe you don't. Call the policeman, we find out. Maybe I call him myself."

"Go right ahead, I ain't got nothin' to hide."

Si waved to Ainsworth. "Find a policeman, bring him here fast. I'll stand here and watch this old highbinder."

The old man looked uncertainly from side to side. "What you want with me?" he quavered.

"I like to know what you workin' at."

"Ain't none of your business!"

Si said with heavy regret, "You know, mister, I don't like to be mean, but you ain't got a leg underneath you."

Ainsworth inquired self-importantly, "You want me to call the cop, Pa?"

"Wait," said Si magnanimously. "I explain things to this old man."

The old man, with weakening determination, said, "I don't need none of your explainin'."

Si thrust his massive face forward. "You know what gonna happen if you don't listen? First, you don't get no more easy ten bucks. That's the easiest thing gonna happen. Second, I call six policemen. They take you to jail, they lock you up, they tie the key on one of them space-rockets. That's the second easiest thing gonna happen to you. Third, you ol' black bastard, I gonna beat you so bad you turn white. You hear me now?"

The old man blustered feebly, "Sure I hear. It don't cut any ice with me. You way off."

"Think of them three bad things," said Si grimly. "No more easy pickin's, that bad old jail, and me."

"Who you?" demanded the old man.

"I'm one of the people you been usin' the mails to defraud. I just don't take it on my back. I get up and fight."

The old man gave up. "I don't know that I'm doing anything wrong. But I was told not to say nothing to nobody."

"And you think you ain't doin' wrong?" sneered Si. "You old, but you ain't dumb."

"No, I ain't dumb," raged the old man. "I never done nobody wrong in my whole life. I ain't gonna start now."

"Start talkin', old man."

"Ain't nothing to talk about," the old man grumbled. "A few months back I get this phone call. The man tells me what to do. He's sendin' me a key. I take it, open this box. In the tan envelope I find ten dollars with another envelope. I mail all the letters. I don't show the envelope to anybody. I don't talk to anybody. Never. At no time. If I do I lose the ten-spot. I'm on the welfare, I need the money. I don't hurt nobody."

"Maybe, maybe not. Who you send the letters to?"

"I don't know."

"Look here, old man —"

"I tell you I don't know!"

"I guess you never look at the address. You never wondered where you was sending all those letters."

"It don't do me no good to look. First place, my eyes ain't so good. Anything I hold in my hands is fuzzy-like. Second place, even if I was to see it I couldn't tell you nothing. I don't read too good."

"Oho," muttered Si. "Can't read."

"I never had no schoolin'. Always too busy makin' a livin'."

Si drew himself up. "I tell you, old man, what I'm gonna do. I'm gonna let you go. Just one thing more. How you supposed to tell this man if things go wrong?"

The old man looked uneasily to the side. "I got ways."

"What ways?"

"Well — maybe you right. Sounds just a little suspicious. I hope I ain't got tangled in something bad."

"What ways?"

"Well, I'm supposed to leave the porch light on all night if anybody bothers me."

"Leave it off, hear? Don't you give no sign."

"I don't like to do that. I said —"

"I don't care what you said. When you come back here?"

"Next week."

"Hah. Next week I gonna come here too. We both look at these envelopes."

"I don't like to do that," said the old man hollowly.

"Mister, nobody come up and ask what you like. I come up and told you what is to be."

The old man went off by himself, bent and muttering in shame. Si strutted back to the balloon-fendered old Buick, Ainsworth loping behind. Si delayed starting the car long enough to light a cigar. He blew a blue cloud toward the sun-visor and clapped Ainsworth on the back. "I'm gonna pay you some money." He fetched out his bulging old wallet, with great deliberation opened it and removed a bill. "Here you go. Lucky two bucks. Take it. It's all yours. But don't tell Vinnie I give you money, hear?"

"Yeah man."

Si pressed the starter. The Buick roared into life, swung out into the street trailing a majestic plume of smoke.

Shaw asked, "The next week, what happened then?"

Ainsworth said woodenly, "Weren't no next week."

"How come?"

"We didn't go."

"Oh? Why not? I thought your pa was hot to see the letters."

"He was hot all right," said Ainsworth. "He was so hot he was just about dead."

"How is that?"

"Somebody run into him, run him down. He just been a little bit out of the hospital."

Chapter IX

Clyde Morrissey, George Shaw

Detective-Inspector Clyde Morrissey was a neat and fastidious man of fifty, with a long fragile jaw, streaked gray hair. His gaze was direct and inquiring; some considered it supercilious in spite of a manner which was mild and quiet. A demoted subordinate had once characterized Morrissey as 'That mizzuble two-bit egghead', although Morrissey's claims to intellectualism were slight indeed; he merely read the weekly news-magazines. Morrissey never smiled, but neither did he become excited. His office was unobtrusively modern, with a desk of gray metal rather than the traditional cigarette-scarred oak. The walls were painted a clean blue-gray; a grass rug covered the liver-brown linoleum.

Reporting to Morrissey on the morning of Monday, June 13, Shaw took a seat on one of the straight-backed chairs. Leisurely he charged and ignited his pipe.

Morrissey leaned back and asked in his uninflected voice, "How's it going?"

"To be honest," said Shaw, "I don't know."

Morrissey made no comment.

"I've worked up a considerable body of information," said Shaw, "but I'm not so sure how much bears on Mr. Big and Paul Gunther's death…" He drew on his pipe. "I've established the method by which Mr. Big collects his loot. It's mailed to a post office box, picked up, presumably once a week, and re-mailed. The man who does this is an illiterate. He doesn't know the second address. This information, incidentally, comes from a man named Si Bethea. Bethea staked out the post office box, watched for the collection. He saw it. Shortly after he got hurt — bad. Hit-and-run victim."

"Suggestive."

Shaw nodded. "Mr. Big apparently comes down to watch the pick-up, to make sure nobody interferes or makes contact with his man. It's his safety-valve."

"Clever set-up," said Morrissey. "But we could crack it. With a man behind the counter to pick off the address on the second mailing."

"I doubt it," said Shaw. "He'd have another safety-valve somewhere. Now, after Gunther's death, for sure. Maybe somebody to pick up the second mail."

Morrissey drummed his fingers on the desk. "All this tells us something about Mr. Big."

"In what way?"

"It indicates that Mr. Big is in a class apart from the typical Seventh Street hoodlum. Imagine Suitcase Simpson working this racket. How would he collect? He'd send around a runner. Mr. Big operates more carefully. No one knows him, he makes contact with nobody. He must have a reputation to lose. Possibly a white man."

Shaw shrugged dubiously. "Not too many white men have the connections. Mr. Big knows everything that's going on."

"Still it might be a good idea to keep this point in mind," said Morrissey, in his driest accents.

"Right." Shaw relit his pipe. "I've really got two lines going at once — one on Paul Gunther, the other on Si Bethea. Both seem to have got close to Mr. Big, and both got hurt."

Morrissey laced his fingers, placed the knuckles under his chin. "Still no lead to Gunther's residence?"

"We're getting there. A little more digging should pay off. But now I don't know what we'll have when we find out. His briefcase isn't so important, because we know generally where he went Friday."

"Generally, but not precisely. Apparently he discussed Mr. Big with someone other than the people you've interviewed. Unless they're lying." Morrissey watched Shaw sidelong. "Gunther's car has turned up, parked on Adair between Eleventh and Twelfth. A citation for reckless driving in the glove compartment."

"Well, well," said Shaw. "Adair — one block west of Lily. Is that where he lives?"

"Apparently not. The patrolman who found the car checked the block."

"The citation — when was that issued?"

"Three-thirty on the afternoon of Saturday the fourth. I've talked to Robinson, the officer responsible. He says Gunther came dashing out of a side road onto Skyline Boulevard, nearly ran him over the edge."

"Hmm. Was Gunther alone?"

Morrissey nodded.

"Odd," said Shaw. He ruminated a moment, chewing on his pipestem. "We've tapped all our sources in West Oakland. No information. Nobody likes to talk about him. After this killing Mr. Big is big league."

"These things grow," said Morrissey. He nibbled his knuckles. "What's on for today?"

"Same general program. Nobody's told me all they know."

"Surprised?" asked Morrissey, gently sarcastic.

"To a certain degree," said Shaw placidly. "So far as Barbara Tavistock is concerned."

Morrissey, a notorious misogynist, snorted. "They're the worst of the lot."

Shaw frowned at his pipe, knocked it out. "I want to talk to Gally Bethea, and Si Bethea. I'd like to take Jeff Pettigrew back over the business of the house on Lily Street. Then there's this character Jim Connor. People seem to think Gunther had a grudge against him."

"Jealousy over the girl?"

"Hard to say."

"It's a peculiar case." Morrissey admitted. He put his palms down flat on the desk-top; reading the signal Shaw rose to his feet. "Anything else?" asked Morrissey. "Need any help?"

Shaw considered. "Gunther apparently has been living somewhere west of Van Buren Avenue. Ted Therbow tells me that Gunther used to drive into his station from Ninth Street. We might make an area check to pick up Gunther's residence."

Morrissey's lips drooped a trifle. "Try Gally Bethea first. If you don't make out there, we'll start the check. Any other ideas?"

"Might ask neighbors something more about the house where Gunther got killed. It's a big question-mark in the case so far. Why in thunder did Gunther pick up the keys to this house?"

"I'll go along on that." Morrissey made a note. "What else?"

"There's the post office. The clerk who services the boxes might have noticed something."

"Long chance. We can try." Morrissey made another note. "Anything more?"

"Maybe a check into Pettigrew's finances. He's from a society background. Why is he with this fly-by-night realtor? Loot? What kind of loot? Is he a big spender?"

"Okay." Morrissey wrote. "Anything else?"

Shaw considered. "Nothing for just now."

Shaw took his leave and drove to the Welfare Department. He found Hubbard standing by the window looking listlessly into the street. The big pale face hung lax, the pink mouth drooped. He turned as Shaw came in, raised his hand in an unconvincingly jaunty salute. "Have a seat, Lieutenant." He went to his desk, settled with a petulant grunt into his own chair. "I suppose there's nothing new?"

Shaw regarded him a moment before answering. Hubbard looked as if he had not slept well. "Not too much," said Shaw.

Hubbard gave his head a dismal shake, avoiding Shaw's eyes. "This business is getting me down."

"So?" Shaw brought out his pipe again. "Why should it affect you?"

Hubbard held up his hands. "Which way is the thing going to blow up? That's what's getting me — the uncertainty of it. So far the papers have treated us pretty well — but you never know."

Shaw nodded wisely, as if he fully comprehended Hubbard's meaning.

"It's the usual story," Hubbard went on. "We need more money, more personnel. It's chronic with us. But we're on the hot spot. Every time there's some little dust-up, we run into trouble. Welfare frauds... Now this Mr. Big affair."

"Aren't they part and parcel of the same thing?"

Hubbard looked up truculently. "Suppose they are, what of it? We know people are cheating us. It's no secret. We try to hold it down to reasonable levels. Then some unspeakable creature like this Mr. Big comes along, cheating the cheaters. There's publicity, the Department looks silly, and our whole public relations program is shot to hell."

Shaw puffed on his pipe. "You seem to have your troubles, like everybody else."

Hubbard slouched morosely back on his chair. "I suppose we're living in a predatory society. I like to think differently, but sometimes it gets me down." He roused himself, studied Shaw sharply. "Surely you've learned something since yesterday?"

Shaw nodded. "I've interviewed the people Gunther saw on Friday. Nobody had anything definite to report. Mr. Big seems to be tapping at least three of them."

Hubbard winced. "Sixty percent. It can't be typical." He sat up in the chair, displaying something of his normal energy. "This whole affair is absolutely fantastic! When I think what the sensational press will do to us —" he shook his head.

"Wait till we catch Mr. Big," said Shaw cheerfully.

Hubbard shuffled the papers on his desk. "Sometimes it's better to let sleeping dogs lie," he muttered.

Shaw raised his eyebrows. "Mr. Big is hardly a sleeping dog. Gunther hasn't even been buried yet."

"True enough. But... I suspect Mr. Big will be lying mighty quiet for a while."

Shaw frowned. "I don't quite understand you, Mr. Hubbard. You're not suggesting that we abandon the investigation?"

"No, no, of course not." Hubbard sighed. "Let the chips fall where they may."

"Strange that you mentioned Mr. Big lying low," said Shaw. "Mr. Big's victims all seem to have received letters instructing them to make no further payments."

"Well, well. I suppose that's encouraging."

"It's interesting," said Shaw. He looked out into the clattering main office. "May I use a telephone for a few moments?"

"Of course. Use mine, if you like."

"I don't want to inconvenience you, Mr. Hubbard. If there's a place somewhere out of the way—"

Hubbard was on his feet, flushing slightly. "I've some business upstairs, you won't be disturbed here."

Chapter X

James Connor

Shaw telephoned the Registrar's Office at the University of California in Berkeley, which supplied him the address and telephone number of James Glenn Connor of Santa Barbara, graduate student in astronomy. Shaw next called the Tavistock residence in Piedmont. The maid answered. Shaw asked to speak to Barbara, and when she came on the line, inquired if she planned to be at home during the day.

Barbara said in a distrait voice, "Yes, I'll be home — although I've told you everything I know."

Shaw said politely, "There may be a few things you've forgotten, Miss Tavistock."

"Oh." There was a pause, "You know then."

"Know what?"

Barbara made no immediate answer. Then she said swiftly, "I really don't want to talk to you today."

Shaw laughed. "Come now. I'm not as vicious as all that."

Barbara asked cautiously, "It's about — Paul?"

"Naturally."

"My father wants to be here if you come."

"That's something you'll have to work out for yourself. If your father wants to be present I've no objection."

"But I do. He's very dense, in some ways."

Shaw said in a matter-of-fact voice, "I'll call at your home this morning. If you want to notify your father, you're certainly welcome to do so."

Barbara said, "Could I meet you somewhere? If you come here, he'll know about it."

"I'll meet you anywhere you say."

"No," said Barbara in sudden decision. "I'll call my father. If you'll come at twelve he'll be here."

"Very well. I'll be there at twelve."

Shaw hung up, and leaned back in his chair, chewing on his pipestem. Then he leaned forward and telephoned the residence of James Connor.

The bell rang, rang, rang. Shaw was about to hang up when a surly voice said, "Hello."

"James Connor?"

"Yes. Who's this?"

"Lieutenant George Shaw, Oakland Police Department. Can you spare me a few minutes this morning?"

"What for?"

"I'm investigating the death of Paul Gunther."

"I'll be here for a while, if you care to drop over," said Connor grudgingly.

"Fine. I'll try to make it inside a couple hours."

"Okay." Shaw heard a click, and the line went dead. He went to the door, looked up and down the office. Hubbard was nowhere in sight. Shaw took his leave.

He drove out Seventh Street, turned north on Van Buren Avenue, stopped in front of the Bethea house. He walked up the concrete path, past the dusty palm trees, climbed the steps, but already he knew the house was untenanted.

He rang the bell, knocked, then went back down the steps. He stood for a moment on the haggard lawn, with the palm leaves rattling and clashing above him. He looked diagonally across the street, to the old house on Lily Street; weather-beaten, ramshackle, probably never to be lived in again. The question recurred: *Why had Paul Gunther come to this house on the night of Sunday, June 5th*?

A pair of children came along the sidewalk, the girl in a crisp white play-dress, the boy in blue jeans and a cowboy hat. They stopped in front of the murder house, stared, murmured together.

Shaw crossed the street. "Hello," he said.

The two looked at him, brown eyes earnest in brown faces. "Hello," said the boy.

"That's a scary house," said Shaw.

The children agreed. "A man was killed there last week," said the boy.

"So I hear. I wonder why."

The children looked at the house. The girl said, "Mr. Big killed him."

"Mr. Big, eh? Who is Mr. Big?"

"He's a bad man," said the girl. "He comes out at night."

"And kills people," said the boy.

"The man who was killed lived near us," said the girl.

"Oh?" inquired Shaw. "Well, well, well. Do you know the house he lived in?"

They shook their heads. "We just saw him," said one. "We don't see him any more now."

"Of course not," said the other. "Because he's dead. You don't see dead people."

"Except on television."

Shaw broke into the conversation. "Where do you live?"

"On Corinth Street."

"Number 2626."

Shaw decided against an immediate visit to Corinth Street. Later in the day an hour or so of leg-work would locate Paul's address. Gally Bethea very likely could lead him there directly.

"Goodby," said the boy. "We're going home."

"Goodby," said Shaw. "Be careful crossing streets."

"We will."

Shaw returned to his car, drove along Ninth Street, turned into Corinth. Seventy-five years ago this had been a street of many pretensions. The houses were large and elaborate, with balconies, cupolas, bay-windows, turrets, rococo columns, gingerbread moldings: all the trappings of Victorian elegance. Now paint peeled back, gardens had become dry wildernesses, laundry hung from the balconies. Nevertheless, Corinth Street maintained a certain rakish grandeur. Shaw well understood how Paul Gunther might enjoy a sojourn here.

He drove north to Berkeley. Jim Connor lived in an apartment to the rear of an old brown-shingle house. He responded in leisurely fashion to Shaw's ring, wearing ragged blue jeans and a T-shirt. "Hi. Come in."

Shaw entered a sparsely furnished living room. On the couch sat Barbara Tavistock, hands clenched in her lap.

Shaw greeted her politely. "I'm surprised to see you here, Miss Tavistock. I understood you to say that your father —"

"He doesn't know I'm here and I'm not going to tell him."

Shaw rubbed his chin. "That's all very well, but —"

"Jimmy and I decided to tell you everything we know. It's not very much, and I don't see how it can help you, but it's on my conscience."

Shaw nodded. "I see."

Connor held up an electric percolator. "Coffee?"

"Thanks," said Shaw. "Black."

Barbara spoke rapidly. "I didn't tell you this before, because it puts me in a poor light. I felt foolish, embarrassed; I still do. But that's neither here nor there. I hoped that you'd find Paul's murderer and wouldn't need to talk to me again." She looked at Shaw sidewise, half-expectantly.

Shaw nodded noncommittally, sipped his coffee. Connor seated himself beside Barbara, and watched Shaw with an air of challenge.

Barbara sat brooding. She spoke suddenly. "The same night I first saw Paul, I met Jimmy. He paid no attention to me." She looked sidewise at Connor, reached up, ruffled his already untidy hair. "Paul took a dislike to Jimmy."

Connor frowned. "I wouldn't call it dislike."

"Perhaps not." Barbara chewed her lip. "I suppose it's a matter of integration. Jimmy knows where he's going; Paul was a wanderer."

"No," said Connor, "it's nothing like that at all. I could explain if you're interested."

Barbara looked at Shaw. "I'm interested."

"Go ahead," said Shaw.

Connor poured out more coffee. "He called on me the other night, pretty late. He'd had a few drinks but he wasn't drunk, just exhilarated."

Barbara made a sound of recognition. "He was the same way when I first saw him. He's really rather fascinating like that." She looked accusingly at Connor. "You never told me he came here."

"You never asked."

"Well — why did he come?"

Connor laughed grimly. "He said he wanted to find out what made me tick. I asked, why the sudden interest, was he studying psychology? He banged a bottle of Scotch on the table, and suggested we check it out. So I got some glasses. He took a big jolt, and sat blinking those yellow eyes. He said, 'Connor, you alarm me. I mean just that. If you are "you" — if you are an "I", an individual — the cosmos is thrown in a turmoil. You'd have the distinction of challenging an entire universe — merely by existing. Do you exist?'

"I said, 'You poured out two jolts of that Scotch. You drank one, I drank the other. They're both gone. I guess that answers your question.'

"He said, 'That's the subterfuge Destiny would use to confuse me.'

"I told him I wasn't interested in metaphysics, especially somebody else's, and I asked him if he'd brought the Scotch to be drunk or just for an ornament.

" 'Drink up,' he said. 'In vino veritas.' He poured out the Scotch, watching me kinda foxy. 'So you're interested in your own metaphysics,' he said. 'What do they tell you? How do you regard yourself in relation to the universe?'

"I said that I didn't have too many facts. As if he'd asked me, is there life on the planets of Sirius? I don't even know if Sirius *has* planets. Why blow a skull-fuse? If he could assure me that the planets were there, give me their masses and orbits, show me a few spectrographs — then I'd speculate like mad. I said, 'I'm here. You're there. That's a bottle of Scotch liquor on the table. I deduce another one inside you.'

"He says, 'Pragmatism. You're a pragmatist.' As if he was calling me a cannibal. Then he caught himself up. 'Maybe I'm wrong. If so — then I'm not a very nice person.'

" 'Suppose you're right?' I ask.

" 'Then I'm the Hero — the Thesis! I'm banging my head on the rocks, and the Adversary, the Antithesis — Destiny — is sitting on the porch drinking lemonade and laughing.'

"I know pretty well what he means, but it's a futile business. I pour him some Scotch, but he jumps to his feet and rushes out, saying he's going to extinguish Mr. Big, or something similar."

Connor went to a cupboard, brought forth a bottle and three glasses. "He forgot his Scotch. It's only fair that we take a drink or two now."

Shaw swirled the liquor in his glass. "What else did he say about Mr. Big?"

"That's all about Mr. Big."

"And when did this happen?"

"Friday night."

"This last Friday? Just before he was killed?"

"Correct."

"Well, well."

"Saturday night is even wilder. And he wasn't drunk."

Barbara spoke in a flat voice. "He came up to our house in Piedmont. Mother and Father had gone out to a party, Jimmy and I were sitting by the fire. The doorbell rang, and it was Paul. He looked very — strange. Wild, excited, full of life. And afraid. Very afraid. He spoke in a whisper, and stood close beside the wall. I said 'Hello', and he said, 'Barbara — can I come in?' I let him in, he sat down by the fire. I went into the kitchen for coffee and he came after me." Barbara shuddered. "I was so relieved to have Jimmy there.

"We talked a few minutes. Paul said he was involved in a minor difficulty. He wondered if I could help him. I asked what kind of difficulty? Paul laughed very flippantly. 'There's a man after me,' he said. 'He's trying to find me. If he finds me he'll kill me.'

"I suggested that he go to the police. No, he said, that wouldn't do. He was looking for the man — in fact they were looking for each other.

"I asked if he planned to kill this man when he found him, and he said, 'Certainly. Otherwise he'll kill me.'

"I told him I was sorry, but that I wouldn't help kill anybody. Then he asked if he could use my car. I told him, certainly not. And I couldn't resist a despicable little dig. 'You might try one of your other girl friends.'

"Paul knew what I was talking about. He gave me one of his queer smiles. He said, 'Never mind. Thanks anyway. By the way, do you know where Jeff lives?'

" 'Jeff Pettigrew?'

" 'Yes.'

" 'What do you want with Jeff,' I asked him.

" 'A business deal.'

"I went to look up the address. When I came back I couldn't see him, I thought he'd gone. Then I saw him in the living room, standing in the dark by the window looking out into the garden. Jimmy sat reading a magazine, paying no attention to him." She turned a look of amused indignation toward Connor.

Connor shrugged. "I won't play straight man to anybody."

"Anyway, I stood watching Paul, wondering if someone were really after him." Barbara smiled bitterly. "Using the insights derived from Psych 1A I diagnosed a case of acute paranoia... He came away from the window and asked if he could leave by the back door. I said, 'Of course', and took him out through the kitchen.

"When I came back into the living room, I went to look out the window. And I got a terrible fright. There was a man looking in." Barbara laughed shakily. "Don't ask me who he was. I couldn't see his face or anything about him — just the outline of his head and shoulders. He was a big man — that's all I could possibly say." Barbara leaned back against the wall. "Now I've told you everything. I don't see how it can help — but there it is."

Shaw considered. "It helps. Everything I learn helps." He shook his head. "Gunther seems to have been a strange fellow."

Barbara asked, "Do you think he really was — well, crazy?"

"Not from a legal standpoint. Probably not from any standpoint. He lived a peculiar sort of existence, but he seems completely in touch with reality."

Connor poured himself another shot of Paul's Scotch. "One man's reality is another man's madhouse."

Shaw rose to go. "You're not holding out anything more on me?"

Barbara flushed. "Nothing I can think of. Nothing important, anyway."

"Such as what?"

Barbara shook her head. "There's nothing."

Shaw drove along San Pablo, parked across the street from McAteel Realty.

A new secretary sat at the desk beside the door, a pudgy blonde girl, eyebrows plucked into a startled arch, lips swollen with lipstick. She looked up at Shaw. "Yes sir?"

"I'd like to see Mr. Pettigrew."

"Your name, sir?"

"Lieutenant George Shaw."

"Will you be seated? I'll see if he's in."

But Shaw remained standing, and a moment later Jeff appeared from one of the back rooms. He greeted Shaw warily. "I thought you were done with me, Lieutenant."

"These things take time, Mr. Pettigrew. Is there somewhere we can talk for a few minutes?"

Jeff glanced at his handsome black-faced wrist-watch. "I've got an appointment in ten minutes..."

"I won't bother you now then," said Shaw. "Will you be good enough to drop by my office at headquarters sometime this afternoon? I'll try to be in at three or three-thirty."

Jeff grunted, cleared his throat. "I'll talk to you now."

"That might be more convenient for everyone," said Shaw.

Jeff led the way to his office, a rather shabby little cubicle. He dropped into his chair, motioned Shaw to another, lit a cigarette and exhaled a great puff of smoke. "What's on your mind?"

"The case is beginning to shape up," said Shaw. "I'm rather curious as to your personal relationship with Paul Gunther."

Jeff gave his cigarette a jaunty wave. "There wasn't any. He was just a guy I happened to know."

"You liked him?"

Jeff shrugged his bulky shoulders. "You might say I was indifferent."

"Even after he — to speak bluntly — even after he took your girl friend away from you?"

Jeff sat up in his chair, hair bristling, eyes round and hard. "Where did you ever get a notion like that? He wasn't man enough to cut me out with anybody."

"I'm referring to Barbara Tavistock."

Jeff made a contemptuous sound. "Nice girl — but."

"But what?"

"Just 'but'. The school-girl type. Sweet co-ed. I like rare meat."

"I see," said Shaw. "So you harbored no antagonism toward Paul Gunther?"

Jeff stared at him. "This almost sounds like you consider me a suspect. You're way off the rails, Lieutenant."

"Just answer my questions, please."

Jeff's voice became laden with a rasping overtone. "Let's get this straight, Lieutenant. I don't like odd-balls. Gunther was way out in left field."

"So you didn't like Gunther."

"Exactly. Nor did I dislike him. I saw him around, I was polite to him. Anything more?"

Shaw considered. "Paul came to see you here Saturday."

Jeff's voice carried a burden of patronizing patience. "I've told you as much."

"What about Friday night?"

Jeff's eyes once more became hard and bright. "What about Friday night?"

"Did you see Gunther Friday night?"

"He dropped in for a few minutes, yes. What of it?"

Shaw smiled. "You failed to mention it before."

"It seemed completely unimportant."

"We like to know these things. What did he want?"

"He came to inquire about that house on Lily Street. He asked if we were acting for the owners. I told him that we had the exclusive and that I'd take him around the next day. Money is money, from your friend or your worst enemy."

"That's all then?"

Jeff's eyes shifted. "He came around the next day like I told you."

"And that's the last you saw of him?"

"That's the last I saw of him."

Shaw was watching Jeff carefully. Jeff defiantly dragged on his cigarette, blew smoke through his nostrils.

"There's nothing else you can tell me?" Shaw asked softly.

"That's all," said Jeff, with a quick twist of his mouth.

Liar, thought Shaw.

There was another pause. Shaw asked, "I suppose you know West Oakland pretty well?"

"Sure. I do a lot of business with blacks. Why do you ask?"

"You told me that Paul Gunther took the keys to the house on Lily Street, that you did not go there yourself."

"That's what I told you and that's the way it was!"

"You've never entered this house?"

"Never." Jeff ground out his cigarette. "Don't tell me you found my fingerprints around the place, because I know you didn't."

Shaw rose to his feet. "For now," he said, "that's all."

Jeff remained seated, exuding antagonism. He reached for a sheaf of papers and became interested in the matters contained therein.

Shaw smiled faintly. "So long, Jeff."

Jeff nodded brusquely, and went back to his work.

Shaw returned to the street. For a moment he stood in the warm sunlight, looking up and down San Pablo Avenue. Jeff Pettigrew was not telling all he knew about the death of Paul Gunther. Shaw was neither indignant nor disillusioned. When private citizens, short of persuasion by rack, red-hot pincer or the knout, told everything to the inquiring police officer, that would be the dawning of the Golden Age.

Shaw turned west off San Pablo, headed toward Van Buren Avenue.

Chapter XI

Gally Bethea

Shaw pushed open the creaking iron gate, passed under the rasping palms, mounted the front porch of the Bethea house. Vinnie answered the bell. She made no pretense of pleasure at the sight of Shaw. "Oh, you again."

"Yes," said Shaw. "Me again. Where's your step-daughter? I want to talk to her."

Vinnie said querulously, "Girl ain't feelin' good. You gotta talk to her today?"

"Yes, Mrs. Bethea. I'm sorry, but it's necessary."

Vinnie grudgingly moved aside. "She don't want to talk to nobody. But I guess that don't make no difference."

"None whatever."

Gally sauntered down the stairs, wearing a black skirt and cinnamon-brown blouse.

"Hello, Mr. Lieutenant," said Gally with magnificent lassitude. She turned to Vinnie. "Any coffee goin' on out back?"

"There sure ain't!" snapped Vinnie. "You want coffee, you know how to make it."

"Rats," said Gally. "This ain't livin'. What do you want, Mr. Lieutenant?"

"I want a nice long talk, Gally. I want you to tell me a few things. The truth this time."

"Why not? I've told you the truth before."

"Not very much of it."

"What I didn't tell you don't matter." She took Shaw's arm. "Come along, buy me some coffee. If we talk in the house that old woman listens to everything."

"Well I never!" cried Vinnie furiously. "After all I done for you and you act like that! Don't you come wantin' things from me, Galatea Bethea! No more! Nothing! You hear? Talkin' like that in front of a stranger! And the condition you in!"

Gally went to the door. "Come on, Mr. Lieutenant. Let's go where there's less trash around."

Shaw, not displeased, took Gally to a nearby drive-in, ordered coffee. He settled back, looked Gally over. "So you're pregnant."

"Just a little bit," said Gally.

"Paul?"

She nodded demurely.

Shaw made a cynical sound. "Last time we talked you didn't mention knowing Paul quite so well."

"I guess not." Gally sipped her coffee. The knuckles shone white through her golden-bronze skin. Shaw speculated as to the cause of her nervousness. "Well — how did it all start?"

Gally shrugged. "Paul came round one day, said he wanted to move out to this neighborhood. I told him, 'Man, you're crazy. This is slums, when you got a nice place in Berkeley?' He said he liked it here, liked some of the chicks. He was talking about me. I didn't care. I liked Paul. I won't say he was a knight in white armor, but — well..." Her voice trailed off. She sipped her coffee. "I knew a little place up on Corinth Street that was going to be vacant — a kind of a remodeled garage back of one of them big houses. I took him up there, he rented it.

"About this time Pa gets run over and they take him to the hospital. Everybody thinks he's done for. Vinnie don't care, it's all right with her. She tells me if Pa dies she's gonna take Ainsworth and live with her sister, and put me in the Juvenile Home."

"That sounds pretty rough," said Shaw.

Gally shrugged. "Ainsworth is her boy. I ain't no relation to Vinnie. I sure don't want to go to no home, so I'm pulling for Pa. He don't die. Too mean, I guess. He just lies there, thinking hard thoughts. That's what keeps him alive, thinking how much trouble he can make for people. Oh he's a mean man." Gally shook her head in rueful admiration. "When Pa kept breathin' Vinnie still figured she'd go visit her sister with Ainsworth. That's down in San Jose. She didn't care what happens to me. She says, 'You stay in this house. When the Welfare Man comes you just say I'm out for a while. If he makes trouble you call me on the telephone.' And she says, 'Just don't go gettin' in trouble; I don't want no reflection against my name!'

"I say okay, suits me. And when Vinnie goes, I move in with Paul. A month goes by, and part of the second month..."

Paul, stretched out on the couch, looked around the room with satisfaction. In the kitchenette Gally was frying hamburgers. All Paul could see was her pert little rump, moving and jerking as she worked.

Paul raised his head, sipped sherry from the glass he held on his chest. At first sight the cottage had dismayed him, had seemed utterly unlivable. But Gally, by the simple act of gathering up two or three armloads of newspapers, magazines, and assorted trash and taking them to the incinerator, had somehow committed him to renting the place.

Everything had worked out fine. They had painted the walls pale blue, the ceiling white; the landlord had furnished pink linoleum tile, which Paul and Gally had laid down. They had bought an old couch, three campaign chairs, a second-hand bed, an unfinished chest of drawers, two reed mats. Gally had been a great help, thought Paul; how could he have managed without her? She was cheerful, easy to get along with; in bed she was sheer delight. Paul thought of Barbara. What would she say if she knew the situation? Paul sipped his sherry. Gally was Gally; Barbara was Barbara. Their worlds had no point of contact. Except himself. Lord knows he'd never bring them together. Gally suspected the existence of Barbara; Barbara naturally had no inkling of Gally. The situation amused Paul. He drained the glass, reached to the floor for the bottle, poured himself a refill. From the kitchen came the sound of sizzling hamburgers.

Everything had worked out beautifully. With Si Bethea in the hospital, Vinnie in San Jose, it had been the most natural thing in the world for Gally to move in with him. A situation both enjoyed, without guilt or misgivings. Only once, on a Saturday morning, after breakfast, with Paul blowing discords on a newly purchased recorder, had Gally become restless. She padded from couch to the window, looked out into the dingy yard, swinging her arms, jingling her copper bracelet.

Paul looked fretfully up from his book of instructions. The recorder was not quite so simple to play as the salesman had suggested. "What's the trouble? You act like a bug trying to get out of a jar."

Gally laughed. "I'm nervous. Silly, I know. Silly me. I keep thinking I oughta be home. Suppose the Welfare Man shows. Then I remember he can't, because Paul's the Welfare Man."

"It's a job," said Paul.

"How long you gonna keep this job?"

"Search me. When I learn to play this instrument, maybe I'll sign with the New York Philharmonic."

"Now Paul. Be serious."

"I'm never serious."

Gally came to sit beside him. She laid her dusky arm beside Paul's pale one. "Butterscotch syrup and vanilla ice cream," said Gally.

"They go good together."

Gally made a sad little sound. "Not really... I wish I was white. I really do. Everything's so easy if you're white."

"White people aren't any happier. They just have different problems."

"You don't know how it is," said Gally. "Look at me. You think I'm pretty?"

"Naturally."

"You know why? Because I got about a third white blood. From my mother. Si's just plain nigger. My mother was a pretty woman. No good though. She's down in L.A., works as a beauty operator. Calls herself Rita Alvarez, says she's from Brazil... Let's go to Brazil, Paul."

"I'd like to. What'll we use for scratch?"

"Can't you get some kind of travelin' job? Like the Diplomatic Service?"

"I might join the Foreign Legion," said Paul. "How'd you like that?"

"You're just teasin', Paul. I'm serious. Brazil's supposed to be real mellow. Fine music, good climate, big steaks for twenty cents, everybody nice to everybody else."

"That's Argentina where you get the twenty-cent steaks."

"I don't care. Let's save up, Paul. I'll get a job. Then we'll buy an old house, fix it up and sell it. Lots of people do it." Gally became so enthusiastic her whole body quivered. "Right across from Pa's place is an old house, on the corner of Lily Street. We could get it cheap, I know for sure. Then in a year or two —"

Paul ruffled her hair. "What a dreamer."

"It's not dreaming, Paul. We could do it for real."

"That place is just a shack. It's not worth fixing up."

Gally sighed, pressed against him, nuzzled his neck. "I might as well."

"Might as well what?"

"Dream."

"Sure. Dream on. It's cheap."

Gally rose to her feet, went back to the window. Paul picked up the recorder.

Now Gally came in from the kitchenette with the hamburgers and a bag of potato chips. She set them on the card-table which served as a dining table. Paul hauled himself to his feet, went out into the kitchenette, took a couple cans of beer from the refrigerator, opened them, brought them back into the living room.

They ate in a silence which presently struck Paul as extraordinary. He looked across the table at Gally. She sat, her head turned down, chewing listlessly. Paul presently asked, "Why the long face? Your Pa worse? Or better?"

"I guess he's all right."

"What's the trouble? You need some money?"

She shook her head. "Paul."

"Well?"

She nibbled on a hamburger. "I'm pregnant."

"What!"

She nodded dolefully. "The second month's gone by. It must have happened first thing."

Paul said in a hushed voice, "I thought you'd got yourself a diaphragm."

"I did… But you know. There was one or two times at first."

"Lord, lord."

Gally's fingers fluttered nervously up and down the can of beer. "If I bust loose with a baby they put me in that home for sure."

Paul made a small gesture. "You're sure about — about this?"

"I guess so. I passed my period twice now." Gally began to cry. Tears welled from her eyes, her mouth twisted.

"Now, now, now," said Paul in a distant voice.

"I'm not a bad girl, Paul. I never did this before. I don't want to go to the home. They treat you awful. Like a jail."

"Hell," said Paul with a kind of subdued bluffness. "They won't put you in a home."

"Sure they will. Paul, I got to do something... Get married."

Paul blinked. Gally looked timorously toward him, eyes tear-wet. A sudden burst of knowledge astonished Paul. "You don't mean me!" He laughed hollowly.

"I gotta get married to somebody. It's you who fixed me."

"Gally, look here. I can't get married. I'm not the marrying kind. I couldn't think of getting tied up just now."

Gally said sullenly, "I still got to get married."

"Christ!" sighed Paul. "Look around a little. There's lots of guys just aching to tie up with a sharp chick like you."

Gally glumly nibbled her hamburger. "Not with my belly poochin' out."

Paul's appetite was gone. He went out into the kitchen, opened another can of beer. He sat for a few minutes thinking, then pulled out his check-book, wrote a check. *Pay to the order of CASH the sum of two hundred and fifty dollars. Paul Gunther.* He pushed the check across the table. "There's more if you need it."

Gally looked at the check. "What's this for?"

"An operation. You know where to go?"

Gally shrank back. "I could find out... But Paul, that's bad. Girls die... All kinds of horrible things happen."

"It's a simple operation. The people are mostly regular doctors, making some tax-free loot..."

Gally shook her head dubiously. "I'll ask around. I got a girl friend who knows about these things."

After dinner Paul changed his clothes and went out, on the pretext of visiting his mother. Gally watched him leave with a kind of quizzical cynicism.

Paul spent a rather exciting evening with Barbara. At a small art theater they saw a re-run of Jean-Louis Barrault's *Les Enfants du Paradis*, then dropped into the Steppenwolf on San Pablo for a beer. At a nearby table sat Jim Connor with a red-haired girl wearing black slacks and a black turtleneck sweater. "Look!" said Barbara. "There's Jimmy, the astronomer."

"I couldn't care less."

Barbara studied him carefully, her eyes searching. "You don't like him?"

"He's just a face in the crowd."

"He's anything but that," said Barbara.

Shortly after Paul suggested that they leave.

Parked in front of the Tavistock house he kissed Barbara with considerably more urgency than he had heretofore attempted. Barbara returned no particular fervor. Paul, adjusting to circumstances, abated the intensity of his love-making. Presently he sensed that Barbara was annoyed. He asked, "What's the trouble?"

"I don't know," said Barbara crossly. "I really don't know."

"I guess it can't be anything serious."

"I don't understand you."

Paul was not displeased. "That's no surprise. I don't understand *you*. How can I? We're two different people."

Barbara made a skeptical sound. "I wonder if you really believe that?"

"Of course."

"I wonder... Sometimes you make me feel like a — a —" she struggled to express herself "— some kind of musical instrument, a guitar, that you're amusing yourself with, trying to play. As if you're tuning the strings, then when they don't sound right, you tighten till you're afraid they'll break; so you loosen them again and play discords... That's not quite what I mean, but it's close enough."

Paul laughed. "You're much too subtle for me."

"It's just the other way around," snapped Barbara. "You know perfectly well what I feel at every minute. I know because you adjust so adroitly."

Paul asked in a strained voice, "Is that good or bad?"

"It's a state of affairs."

Paul said with hollow facetiousness, "Then I'm not playing the guitar; the guitar plays me."

"Let's go in," said Barbara.

At the door she turned suddenly, kissed Paul on the cheek. "I'm sorry I'm so cross tonight." She laughed uncertainly. "I don't know what gets into me... I think too much." She kissed him again. "Goodnight."

"When will I see you again?"

"I don't know. Call me."

Paul drove back to West Oakland in a somber mood. He parked in front of the little cottage on Corinth Street, switched off engine and lights and sat in the dark. Barbara was slipping away from him. This was bad. Worse, she had put him on the defensive; he had become annoyed and uneasy; he had been wedged away from the rock-solid basis of the Creed. He repeated Article 2 to himself, and sardonically contrasted his actual performance. Destiny had won a clear-cut, if minor, victory tonight—in fact, across the entire day. Paul thought of Gally. Poor scared kid. Well, he'd got her in trouble, he'd get her out, no matter how much it cost: Article 3. Though if he chose to act by the strict letter of Article 5... Paul grimaced. Destiny of course would win the game at its own time. But not on its own terms.

Considered in this light, his embarrassment with Barbara became a mere incident, Gally's pregnancy no more than a grotesquely amusing mishap. Paul alighted from the car, stood in the street, breathing the cool fog-scented air. The houses raised enormous medieval silhouettes above him, dark along the length of the block except for a few luminous rectangles, arranged with the dramatic artlessness of a stage-set.

Buoyed, stimulated, almost elated, Paul strode down the hydrangea-lush walk to the cottage. Gally looked drowsily up from the bed as Paul came in, and at the expression on Paul's face sighed and stretched voluptuously. Paul threw off his clothes, turned off the light, got into bed.

"Careful," said Gally in a warm husky voice, "don't wake the chile."

Immediately after breakfast Gally left the house. It was another Saturday, and Paul did not work. Late in the afternoon she returned, resplendent in a beautiful suit of beige Shetland tweed, with a matching cashmere sweater.

Paul stared in amazement. Gally trotted gaily across the room, threw her arms around him. "Don't I look nice? Say I look nice."

"You look very nice. Highly nice. You weave all these yourself?"

"Now you just jivin' me, Paul."

"I wonder who's jivin' who?" Paul seated himself on the couch. "What did you find out?"

"About what?" Gally squinted, wrinkled her nose. "Oh, that old thing. I talked to a girl friend. She says it's awful." Gally hunched up her shoulders, shuddered emphatically. "Girls die, maybe they get cancer; their organs get all twisted and swirled up. This girl says they come at you with a big thing like an ice-cream scoop." She shuddered again. "It's scary, Paul. Real scary. Costs an awful lot of money too."

"How much?"

"Oh — three, four hundred. Something like that."

"How much is left of the two-fifty I gave you?"

Gally made no answer. She preened, pivoted, eyeing Paul provocatively. Paul noticed her new alligator pumps.

"You know something, Paul? I could pass. As a Hawaiian. Or a Cuban, maybe."

Paul sighed. "Gally, you're a nice kid. I can't marry you. I don't want to get married. Unless it's some old widow with an enormous fortune."

"You've got one staked out, Paul?"

"I keep looking. When I find her, I got it made."

"Maybe you already found her, Paul. Your mother don't leave lipstick on your shirt. It don't look like expensive lipstick, so maybe she ain't even got a fortune."

Paul stared at her coldly. "You've got a good eye for lipstick."

"Sure. What every girl learns young."

"In any event, it's not any of your concern."

"But it is my concern, Paul! I got to think of myself. You marry me, then you can do what you want. Just so there'll be somebody to help take care of Junior. If I have a baby I want to raise him right. Not back on Van Buren Avenue."

"Gally," said Paul, "I gave you two hundred and fifty dollars. You were supposed to get yourself an operation. Instead you blow the money on clothes. Well, it's done. I'm not worried about money. I'll buy you the operation. But please—"

"No, Paul. I'm scared!"

"—include me out of your plans for the future. It won't work."

Gally flounced over to the couch. "Go get me a beer."

Paul opened two cans of beer, brought them in. Gally gulped. She looked at him across the shiny metal top. "I'm gonna tell Mr. Big on you," she said in a flippant voice, which nevertheless had a brittle edge.

"Oh you are," said Paul. He took a seat beside her. "How are you going to find Mr. Big?"

Gally jerked her shoulders. "I can find him. Black folks all know Mr. Big."

"Now is that right. Who is he then?"

"Something I ain't saying."

Paul laughed, put his arm around Gally. "You're a cute little dickens."

Gally leaned archly back against him. "Here," she said. "Let me take 'em off. You just mess things."

There was no more said about an operation. Intermittently Gally sulked, but Paul refused to notice. On Monday night he telephoned Barbara, who announced that she was busy the entire week, and the week-end likewise. Paul hung up in annoyance. Returning to the cottage he told Gally that next Friday they'd be going to a party, at the house of an artist.

Gally felt thrilled and excited, and wanted to buy a new black dress. Paul said sternly, "First you get that operation. Then things'll be better for both of us."

Shaw signaled the car-hop and ordered more coffee. Gally spoke on in an apathetic voice. "It was a funny thing. We went to this party and I saw how he acted around this Barbara girl. It was really funny. I asked him if this was the girl he was after, with the enormous fortune. He said, of course not, was I crazy?" Gally laughed bitterly. "I was crazy all right. I was crazy to get mixed up with Paul. By this time I was pretty worried, couldn't really think straight. I found out where Barbara lived from a black guy who knew her. Ted Therbow. I telephoned her and asked if I could come talk to her. She said all right, so I went to see her. I guess Paul was right about the fortune, because she lives in a real swanky house in Piedmont. I felt pretty bad. Compared to her I didn't have anything except Paul's baby. And that wasn't worth a thing.

"I gotta say she's a nice girl. She's proud, but not a bit stuck-up. She treated me real nice. I ask her about Paul; she says so far as she's concerned she's done with him. She ain't about to marry him." Gally looked at Shaw. "Did you say something?"

"No. I was just thinking how some people just can't tell the truth."

Gally said in an injured voice, "I'm telling the truth."

"I wasn't thinking of you."

"Oh. Well, anyway, I go home. Paul has a bottle of Scotch out, and he's had a couple drinks. He's not in a good mood, I see that. But like a little fool I spill everything. I tell Paul I happened to see Barbara, that we got talkin'. I never seen him so mad. First he takes a drink of whiskey, then he slaps me twice, good and hard. Then he goes back to the table and looks at me and drinks his whiskey. I wonder what he's up to. I don't like his look. I don't like him any more. I say, 'Paul, what you thinkin' about?' And he says, 'I got a little system which tells me how to win at the Game of Life. I got to figure this thing out.'

"I watch him sitting there and drinking whiskey. He don't care for me, he's just so wrapped up in himself you can't imagine. Not exactly selfish, he's generous with whatever he's got and he's polite... But it's just as if he's doing it for fun and nobody really counts but himself.

"I don't say anything and he don't say anything. He just sits there drinking whiskey and thinking. All of a sudden I get panicky. You know how you always hear of guys killing girls they've got in trouble? I can just see Paul doing this, and so I get up and leave the house. He don't care. He don't pay no attention. I guess maybe he's too drunk now.

"Well, I tell you, talk about shock. I get out on the street, and here comes Pa ambling along Corinth just as big as you please.

"I say, 'Hello, Pa.'

"He says, 'Hello, Gally. I been lookin' for you. I hear you shacked up with a white boy. What did I tell you about things like that?'

"I say, 'It ain't nothing serious, don't make a fuss.'

"He says, 'I ain't fussin'. I do more than fuss. I gonna take my strap to you. Ain't you 'shamed?'

"I say, 'I ain't done nothing so terrible.'

"He wants to know, who is this big-time cat? I ain't got nothing to lose. I say, 'You know him, it's the Welfare Man.' "

Gally smiled wanly. "I really surprise Pa. He just stands and looks at me. Then I say, 'He got me in a family-way, and now he don't want to marry me.'

"Pa looks at me like I'm crazy. He say, 'Gally, you don't have no sense. Course he ain't gonna marry you. You a nigger gal.' That makes me mad. I say, 'I don't care about that — things aren't like the old days. I know lots of mixed couples; they live together just like anybody else.'

"Pa just gives a big laugh. He don't care any more for me than Paul. I think the hell with them both. I think I'll just get this operation first thing and get it over with. I don't want no baby. But Pa grabs hold of me. 'I come lookin' for you. Where you live?' I show him. He says, 'Come along, we go see this big lover-man.'

"Well, I don't care. Makes no difference to me. I take Pa back to the cottage and we go in. Paul's lying on the couch, passed out. He's gone through half a bottle of whiskey.

"Pa don't want me to wake him. He says, 'You just hold your horses. I want to study things over.'

"So I sit down an' Pa rambles the whole house. He find Paul's briefcase. He looks at the initials on the outside and he says, 'Who's this G.P.G.?'

"I say, 'That's Paul. Garnett Paul Gunther, that's his name.' And I say, 'You better not fool with that. It's official U.S. Government business.' Pa says, 'Ain't I a taxpayer? Ain't I a citizen? I got a right to study these things.'

"So he sits down, big as you please, and goes through Paul's things. There's nothing there. I seen Paul working lots of times. Just reports and questionnaires and two or three little manuals and instruction books, things like that. Old Pa looks funny studying these papers. I laugh and he gets mad. I go in the bedroom and lie down and wonder what's gonna become of me.

"I hear Pa get up and I go to the door. He's got Paul's wallet and he's taking Paul's money. I start to yell, but then I think I really don't care.

"Pa is ready to go. He say, 'Come along, you goin' home.'

"I'm scared to go with him. I don't like to be alone with Pa. He never done anything, but I think maybe he got some funny ideas. Besides he say he's gonna take his strap to me. I say, 'I ain't setting foot in that house till Vinnie comes back.' I think Pa is gonna get mad, but he just laughs. He's tickled about something. 'Don't you worry about Vinnie,' he says. 'She come back running when I call her on the telephone.'

"I say, 'You call her then, and maybe I come home tomorrow.'

"He starts to get mad, then he gets up and leaves. Oh, I'm really blue. Paul lying there drunk. I just despise everything in the world. I cry myself to sleep.

"I think it must be about midnight when I hear Paul in the living room. He's muttering and hunting around like a madman. I go take a look. He's got his hair on end, he's wild. He yells, 'Who's been robbing my stuff?'

"I tell him about Pa. I say I couldn't do nothing about it. Paul is mad clean through. He says, 'Clear outa here, I'm done with you.'

"I say, 'It's the middle of the night.' He says, 'Clear out or I throw you out on your fanny.'

"I got mad. I say, 'I need money for my operation.' He flings down in the chair, he writes a check for three hundred dollars. One thing about Paul, he was never stingy. He says, 'Take it and get.' Now I got my pride too. I take the check and I march out with my nose in the air. I never see Paul again."

Gally sighed mournfully. "That was a week ago. I stayed with my girl friend. I ask her about the operation, she say she knows where I can get fixed up. Cost maybe two hundred. I say go ahead, make the appointment." She looked at Shaw in sudden apprehension. "You won't try to stop me?"

Shaw frowned. "I guess I didn't hear anything you said. Just be sure you get somebody reliable."

"My friend says it's a regular doctor."

"Just be sure... Well, what else happened?"

"Oh, nothing much. It was the end of everything for me. I feel now like I'm ninety years old."

Shaw cleared his throat. "I'd say you got out of this mess pretty lucky. I'd make sure I didn't get in another one."

"Oh I really mean to be careful, Mr. Shaw. Really I do. I learned my lesson." Gally nodded with profound determination.

"Getting back to Paul, what happened to the briefcase?"

"I guess it's still there, at Corinth Street. Unless that man took it."

"What man?"

"Oh, some big fat-faced white man."

Shaw looked his puzzlement. Gally explained. "I went there Tuesday night to get my things. There was a man sitting in the house, bold as brass. I walk in and say 'Hello'. I was surprised, because he had Paul's briefcase open on the table, and was going through the papers.

"He say, 'Who're you?', and I say 'Who're *you*!'

"He says, 'If you got to know, I'm with the Welfare Department, and I'm straightening out some business.'

"I thought it was funny Paul leaving his briefcase behind; he was always particular about that briefcase. But I don't care no more. Let the man take everything. I don't say nothing to him. I go into the bedroom, pack my clothes. When I come out he's gone."

"You've never seen this man before?"

"No sir, never."

"He said he was from the Welfare Department. Did you believe him, or did you think he was lying?"

"Oh I guess he was a Welfare man. They kinda get a look after a while. Like they figurin' up if you worth thirty dollars a week to the government to keep alive. Except Paul. He was never like that."

"Just what did this Welfare man look like?"

"Well, he was big in the chest; he got a funny little belly and skinny legs. Big arms, and big hands with long white fingers. His face was big and round, with the eyes and nose and mouth all scrunched in together. He had light brown hair, but not much of it. I think his eyes were blue, or maybe gray. I don't remember much except they were cold and pinched up close together. He had real pale skin, like wax paper. He wore a light brown coat, brown pants; he had big feet like an old rooster, and pointed yellow shoes."

Shaw laughed grimly.

"What's funny?" asked Gally.

"Nothing very much," said Shaw. "Nothing whatever." He tapped his horn, paid the car-hop, started the car.

Gally looked at him uneasily. "Where we going?"

"I want to talk with your Pa. Is he at home?"

Gally shook her head. "He ain't been near home. I know where he hangs out, though."

"Where?"

"If I show you, will you tell him I told you?"

"No."

"Okay. Turn left."

Shaw drove along Beaumont Street to Eighth, turned east. Gally pointed ahead to where the front of an old house had been extended, painted a hideous liver-brown, fitted with windows, a door, soft-drink and beer advertisements. "See that place?"

Shaw read the sign. "'Samphire's Bar-B-Q Hut'—there?"

Gally nodded. "He's either in the back playing poker, or maybe he's sleeping upstairs. That's his hang-out."

"Okay," said Shaw. "Now I'll take you home."

Chapter XII

Si Bethea

Shaw telephoned headquarters, returned to Samphire's. A few minutes later a city car with a pair of plain-clothes men joined him. Shaw sent one to the rear, and entered with the other.

A young woman in a bright blue uniform stood wiping glasses behind the counter. At first she paid them no attention, then scrutinized them with great care. She turned a furtive glance over her shoulder. Following her gaze Shaw saw a young man of eighteen or nineteen eating a hamburger at the end of the counter. A bottle of beer stood half-empty in front of him.

Shaw walked past the counter, investigated the room to the rear, which was furnished as a dining room. He looked around to see the young man who had been eating the hamburger rise to his feet with ostentatious casualness. He started to saunter to the door.

"Just a minute," said Shaw. The plain-clothes man barred the young man's way.

Shaw came forward. "Let's see your driver's license."

"Ain't got none," the young man said in a voice of weary disgust. "Hey, man, what you pickin' on me for? I ain't done nothin'!"

"How old are you?"

"Twenty-one."

Shaw turned to the waitress who was watching in frozen-eyed distress. "Where is Mr. Samphire?"

"He's out in back."

"Is Si Bethea here?"

The waitress blinked. "I don't know no Si Bethea. Who you people anyhow? What you want here?"

Shaw flashed his badge. "You know something? If Si Bethea is here, and you haven't told me, Samphire's going to lose his license." He jerked his head at the glowering youth. "Serving liquor to minors."

"Hell, man, don't be foolish," said the youth in scorn.

The waitress cried in a high-pitched voice, "I just serve beer. That ain't liquor. I don't know how old people is who comes in here."

"You don't know Si Bethea, then?"

The waitress said sullenly, "You mean a big man, big strong man, little bumped-in nose, big chin?"

"If that's Si Bethea, that's who I mean."

The waitress said angrily, "If that's who you mean, he's upstairs."

"What's he doing upstairs?"

"Just talkin'."

"Go get Samphire. Don't talk to anybody else, if you want to keep working here."

"Huh! I don't care if I work or not."

The youth sidled toward the door. The plain-clothes man said, "Hold it, sonny."

"Check him for ID," said Shaw.

"Got a wallet, kid?"

"Naw. Don't carry nothing like that. Don't need it."

Shaw stepped over, patted the back pockets, felt a lump, took out a wallet. Without comment he opened it, found the driver's license. "Howard Ervin Biggleston. Age eighteen. That you?"

"Naw. I'm just carrying it around."

"I see." Shaw returned the wallet. The waitress marched in the room, stepped behind the counter with a vindictive glance toward Shaw. Behind her came a tall cream-colored man of fifty, with long jowls and a tremendous paunch. He looked from Shaw to the plain-clothes man, to young Biggleston, and then accusingly at the waitress. "Ain't I tole you never serve these young punks? Ain't I tole you, obey the law?" He turned to Shaw. "You just gotta 'scuse it, Mr. Policeman. It's something we don't never do in here. We extra careful with the booze. We got a good reputation, you ask anybody—"

Shaw nodded. "I want to see Si Bethea, but I don't want to go finding my own way around your house."

Samphire's pendulous lips fluttered. "Si Bethea?"

"Yes. I want to see him."

Samphire broke out into a sweat. "Who tole you Bethea was here?"

"Never mind who told me. Are you going to take me where he is?"

Samphire laughed in great good-humor. "Sure. You want to see Si, why not? Si ain't done nothing. He's a good friend of mine. We been having a friendly game of cards —"

"You're running a game on the premises too?" Shaw spoke with playful malice, and Samphire grinned back hopefully.

"Just somethin' between friends. Nothin' wrong in that, eh?"

"Come on, Samphire, let's go see Bethea."

Samphire hesitated, swung his big swag of a belly as if planning a protest, then turned and said in a surly voice, "Up the top of the stairs. I ain't gonna take you there."

Shaw jerked his head to the plain-clothes man who released young Biggleston. They passed through the dim little restaurant, climbed bare wooden steps to the second floor. An open door revealed a round table covered with green cloth, with a naked bulb hanging above. Shaw stopped in the doorway, looked around the room.

Five men sat playing poker. Another two looked on. Cigar smoke hung blue in the air, the floor glistened with beer bottles.

Shaw said, "Cash in, Mr. Bethea. I want to have a talk with you."

The game halted abruptly, the players swung around in their chairs, the whites of their eyes showing against dark cheeks.

Si gave no sign that he had heard. Then he said, "What you want with me?"

"You know what we want with you."

Si flung his cards to the table, folded the money in front of him, tucked it deliberately into the breast pocket of his jacket, swept up his loose silver. He put his hands on the table, pushed himself to his feet. He lowered his head and for a long ten seconds stared at Shaw. "Where we goin'?"

"To police headquarters."

"You puttin' me under arrest?"

"No."

"Maybe I won't go then."

Shaw understood that Si was now concerned with saving face in front of his friends. He said, "It's every citizen's duty to help the police, Mr. Bethea. Unless," he added dryly, "there's some reason why you don't care to help us."

Two of the card-players laughed, suppressing their mirth as Si turned to scrutinize them.

Si said in a heavy voice, "Fuzz never done nothing to help me; I don't go too far to help them."

Shaw said nothing, but moved out of the doorway to give Si room to pass. Si stalked forward. At the doorway he turned and said to the card-players, "Don't go 'way with all that money. I be back pretty soon."

Shaw led the way down the stairs; Si followed, grunting at each step; the plain-clothes man brought up the rear.

Si entered the police car with monumental dignity. There was a short wait while the second plain-clothes man was summoned; then they drove away.

"This all silly business," said Si. "You want to know something, why don't you just ask me? Instead you waste all your time, all my time, waste gas, tires wear out. For what? Nothin'. Just plain silly."

"When are you going to start supporting your family?" asked Shaw.

"That what you bringin' me down here for? I ain't got no family. Don't want one. You ain't talkin' about Vinnie?"

"Also Ainsworth and Galatea."

"Shucks. They old enough to watch for themselves."

Shaw made no further comment; the Welfare Department could prosecute for non-support any time they chose. He would be seeing Hubbard today, in connection with another matter... Shaw smiled sadly. It just went to show you could take nothing, ever, for granted.

Si was escorted into the office Shaw shared with Lieutenant Tom Caldwell, and allowed to wait while Shaw drank a leisurely cup of coffee. Shaw returned to find Si thumbing through a *Reader's Digest*.

Shaw seated himself behind his old oak desk. A sergeant positioned himself with pencil and pad at a table across the room. A microphone built into Shaw's desk-lamp fed a tape-recorder in the next room.

Shaw said, "Mr. Bethea, I imagine you know why you are here."

"You still talkin' about my family? Shucks!" Si spoke with disgust. "I never think the city was gonna fool with a little thing like that. Pretty cheap."

"I'm investigating two separate but connected situations: the murder of Paul Gunther, and the extortion practiced by 'Mr. Big'."

Si chuckled. "That Mr. Big he just don't practice. He's good. Nearly kill me off."

"How did that happen?"

Si's glance was cold and haughty. "Ain't you been talkin' to Ainsworth? He spill out his gut, I know that."

"I want to hear it from you."

"Ain't nothing to it. This Mr. Big, he write me a letter, he try to do me for some money. Ha ha! He rasslin' the wrong bear. I told him, go chase yourself, you son of a bitch. Then I got thinking. I wonder who this man can be. So I take Ainsworth and go down to the post office. Well, Mr. Big he's a careful man, he's smart, but I'm smart too. I see this old man come get the mail, and I think, Mr. Big he's gotta be close by. I look around. Lots of people here. Nobody I know. I think maybe next week I try again. So that night I'm down in Samphire's and I get a call on the telephone.

"I say, 'Hello, this Mr. Bethea speakin'.'

"And I hear, 'Si, this Mr. Big. I hear you foolin' around my business.'

"I say, 'I just been checkin' a few things. You make a mistake, Mr. Big. Nobody pulls Si Bethea's britches down. He's too big and mean.'

"He say, 'You mighty wrong, Si. I'm sorry for you. You gonna find yourself in big trouble. People around here call it "Mr. Big Trouble". Mighty tough stuff.'

"I say, 'Mr. Big, I got a proposition for you. I gonna do you a favor. I gonna take you on as a partner.' " Here Si looked sardonically at Shaw. "Of course I don't mean this, I just wanta find out what he say. So I tell him, 'We work this business right. You smart, I'm smart and mean both. We do good.'

"He say, 'Oh I'm mean too, Si. I'm even meaner'n you.'

"I say, 'That's mighty hard, Mr. Big. You better think about my proposition.'

"He say, 'Si, I didn't call for foolishness. You gonna send me my money? You cheatin' the Gov'ment. That's Alcatraz Island stuff.'

"I say, 'I ain't cheatin' nobody but you, Mr. Big. I gonna catch up with you, then look out!' " Si shook his head sadly. "I make my mistake right then. I think this Mr. Big, he ain't foolin' around no man; just these old women. I make my bad move right there. What happens I go play some more poker. Lose twenty, thirty dollars. When I come out, about two o'clock in the morning, I *mad*. I look around. Where my car? It's gone. Look like somebody done clouted my car. I start walkin' home. I cross the street, here comes a car behind me. Just before it hits me, I look. It's my old Buick. Mr. Big run me down with my own car! What you think of that?" He stared at Shaw with indignant red-rimmed eyes.

"Pretty hard," Shaw agreed.

"I wake up in the County Hospital. They all surprise I ain't dead. I lay three months. Mr. Big don't even send me no flowers. Two, three weeks ago they let me out. I think, I gonna catch that Mr. Big. I gonna make him sing."

Si paused, looked pointedly around the room.

Shaw watched him quizzically. "Lost something?"

"I think maybe you got a bottle of whiskey in here. I'd take a drink."

"I'm afraid not. We can't afford to let our suspects get up in court and claim we tried to get them drunk."

Si thrust out his big head menacingly. "Here, you ain't gonna go callin' me no suspect."

"If it offends you," said Shaw, "I'll stop."

Si lurched back in his seat. "You about finished? I got business to tend to."

"No," said Shaw. "I'm nowhere near finished. You haven't hardly told me anything!"

Si shrugged. "Done told you all I know."

Shaw shook his head. "I'm afraid not, Mr. Bethea. There's lots you haven't told me. What happened when you left the hospital?"

Si glared gloomily at Shaw. "I just go on where I left off."

"You went looking for Mr. Big."

Si shook his head. "I figger he leave me be, I leave him be. He too mean to fool with."

Shaw sat back in his chair, studying Si. The face was completely unreadable. The eyes were hard and opaque as beetle-shells, the mouth stiff and heavy.

At last Shaw said, "You told me you were anxious to get out of the hospital so that you could look up Mr. Big."

Si feigned a massive surprise. "I told you that?"

"Yes."

"I guess I change my mind. Nothing wrong with that."

"You went out looking for your daughter instead? Is that it?"

Si maintained an impassive silence.

"You went to the house on Corinth Street, you found her with Paul Gunther."

"Who tole you that?" demanded Si. "Gally tole you that? She lie. She a no-good lyin' lil cur."

Shaw wondered at Si's sudden perturbation. Cautiously he said, "Gally told us a lot more. She says she'll swear to it in court."

"She lie."

Shaw turned to the sergeant. "You're taking all this down?"

"Yes sir."

"Don't make no difference to me," said Si. "Just talk. Talk don't hurt nobody."

Shaw leaned back in his chair. "Gunther was asleep. You —"

"He drunk," snorted Si.

"— went through his briefcase. You took money from his wallet."

"He ain't kickin' about it."

"No. He's dead." Shaw rose to his feet. Si watched him suspiciously.

"Let's go," said Shaw.

"Where we goin'?"

"Down to the desk. I'm booking you on a larceny charge."

Si slowly rose to his feet. "You makin' a big mistake."

"How so?"

"It's no good makin' trouble for Si Bethea."

"You're threatening *me*?"

Si grinned widely. "Don't go tellin' me what I say."

"Let's go," said Shaw shortly.

He led the way, through the door, along the long cheerless corridor.

From behind came a hoarse choking sound, a scrape of feet. Shaw whirled. Si and the sergeant scuffled in the corridor. At Si's feet lay a big black wallet. The sergeant hung to one of Si's arms, Si beat at the sergeant with his other arm, meanwhile bobbing his head at a fragment of paper in his constricted fist, snapping at it with his teeth. Shaw sprang behind Si, threw one arm around his neck, locked Si's free arm, pulled him back. "Drop it," he snarled. "Drop it or you'll get hurt!"

Si kicked backward, Shaw pulled his legs to the side; the sergeant hit Si's fist with the barrel of his revolver. Si's fingers opened; the wad of paper dropped to the floor. Si tried to stamp on it. Shaw pulled him back, the sergeant snatched up the paper.

"All right, Si," said Shaw. "That's all. Unless you'd like a good rap on the sconce."

Si shuddered like a winded horse. His shoulders sagged. Shaw said to the sergeant, "Check him over."

Gingerly the sergeant patted Si's pockets. From Si's back pocket he drew a heavy clasp knife with a six-inch blade.

"Okay," said Shaw. "Back to the office. We'll see what you were trying to lose."

"Ain't nothin'," rumbled Si. "You wanta arrest me, go ahead. Just don't make all this filly-faddlin'."

"This way, Mr. Bethea," said Shaw suavely. "If you please."

Back in the office, Si settled sullenly in the chair. He pulled out a cigar, spat off the end, set it alight with clumsy fingers.

Shaw spread open the paper. It was a sheet of lined three-hole notebook filler. A careful hand had drawn a line down the middle and on each side had noted perhaps fifty names and addresses.

Shaw looked up. "Did you write this?"

Si looked out the window, blew a contemptuous plume of cigar smoke toward the ceiling. Shaw smiled grimly, returned to the list of names. Halfway down he saw the name *Wilma Smith,* and a little further *Angelo Laverghetti.*

Shaw looked at Si, who seemed very thoughtful. "Well, Mr. Bethea, we're commencing to make some headway. This seems to be a list of Mr. Big's clients."

"You sayin' I'm Mr. Big?" demanded Si.

Shaw turned to the sergeant. "Let's look at that knife."

The sergeant laid the knife on the desk. Si scratched his head, rubbed his chin.

Shaw opened the knife, brought out a magnifying glass, put his eye close to the blade. He looked up. "I think there's dry blood in the joint, Mr. Big. We'll check it in the laboratory. If it's human blood, and if it corresponds to Paul Gunther's blood type, you're in pretty bad trouble."

Si shook his head emphatically. "I ain't Mr. Big. No sir!" He slouched back in his seat. "All right. I tell you how things went. I tell you everything. The whole works. I don't hold nothin' back. Then I ask you, what would you do if you was me?"

"Okay," said Shaw. "Let's hear the truth for a change."

With exaggerated care Si tipped the ash from his cigar into the ashtray on Shaw's desk. "This the way things go. Like I tell you I come out of the hospital. I still sore and stiff. I ain't no young rooster like I was ten, twenty years ago. But I still pretty much a man. I come home. No Gally. I go lookin' for her; there the lil bitch shackin' with the Welfare Man. I sure don't think much of that. I go in the house. He's drunk — passed out I guess. Gally she tell you what happen.

"Well, next day, that's Thursday, I go to the telephone, and I make a telephone call. I say, mighty nice-like, 'Mr. Big, this Si Bethea talkin' here. I think you and me better do business.'

"He say, 'I don't know what business you mean.'

"I still talk nice and calm. I say, 'Mr. Big, you put me in the hospital. I lay there three months, thinkin' that when I come out Mr. Big he'll do right and pay me my money. Otherwise it's too bad for Mr. Big.'

"Now he gets mad. He say, 'Si, I thought you was smart. You don't act like you smart. You make one fool move, I gonna kill you. I gonna kill you dead as mackerel. You gonna be lyin' on a cold slab, your eyes like boiled eggs.'

"Now I get mad. I say, 'White boy, you run me down, you bust my bones. You get into my girl, you knock her up, now you say you gonna kill me. That ain't how things is gonna be. I tell you the difference. I gonna kill you. That's gonna be the difference. I gonna make a real habit of it. Please don't run outa town, I wanta see you bad!'

"He don't say no more. The telephone line sings like he's thinking.

I can hear all them typewriters clackin' behind him. I figger now he's scared, maybe now he'll pay me my money. Of course I just bluffin', talkin' big. Then he hangs up the phone quiet-like. I know I got him scared. I got him *too* scared." Si shook his big head sadly. "I just plain foolish, because I know what he does before. He does it again. I come back to Samphire's about three o'clock that afternoon. I cross the street and — *whoosh!* Big car come bustin' right at me. Just like before. Only it ain't my car. And this time I kinda on the lookout. That Mr. Big he miss me so close he knock the ash off my cigar. Now I get mad. I jump in my Buick, go out after him. He don't see me, he thinks nobody on his tail. I foller him, he comes to MacArthur Boulevard, he stops at the stop-light. I look; here comes a big truck lickety-split. I get behind him, I put 'er in low, I feed the gas. I push his car right out in traffic. He gives a big twist, the truck gives a big twist, they don't hit. That man he scared. He look around. Now he knows I'm after him. I know he after me." Si held out his hand in a gesture of helpless resignation. "I don't like it. But what should I do? That man he chasin' me down."

"You could have come to the police," said Shaw. "That's what we're here for."

Si blinked, as if this were a totally novel concept. He shook his head and spoke in a tone of gentle raillery. "I know them police. They say, 'Mr. Bethea, please don't plague us now. We got important business. Nobody tryin' to hurt you. Go home, we be much obliged.' "

Shaw laughed. "If you'd told the police, naturally you wouldn't be able to muscle into Mr. Big's racket."

"You sayin' that, not me."

Shaw shook his head, marvelling. "A fine pair of rogues. Neither one of you daring to go to the police."

"Here now," blustered Si. "You ain't got no right callin' me names."

Shaw made a weary gesture. "Go ahead. You tried to push him in front of a truck. He got away. Then what?"

Si rubbed his chin, working the corners of his mouth up into a wolfish grin. "All right. I tell you how it was. He huntin' me, I huntin' him. So now the fun begins. We run all over town. I say this about that man. He's like a rattlesnake. He's smart and mean. I never know just how I stand..."

*

Paul felt nothing but astonishment at the impact from the rear, the lurch out into opposing traffic. His heart hammered in his windpipe. The truck which had missed him careened down the street, the driver wrestling for control, no doubt cursing passionately. The rear-view mirror revealed a bulge-fendered Buick, an anonymous form hulked over the steering-wheel.

Paul's frantic effort had swung him at right angles to his original course. He now shakily accelerated to keep pace with the traffic. Behind came the Buick. Paul became burningly angry, and his alarm receded. Watching in the mirror he noticed the Buick maneuvering to get behind him once more. Paul smiled a taut smile. No harm could come of that, unless Paul were so rash as to stop again at an intersection in the front rank of cars.

Paul drove carefully, shifting lanes as often as the Buick pulled up behind him. This was a game two could play, and who could doubt the issue? He thought of the Creed, of Article 6, and sat straighter in the seat. Act, rather than react... Paul turned right at University Avenue, right again at Grove Street. He made no effort to evade the Buick; this was no particular problem: if he chose, he could merely cruise back and forth until the smoke-belching old Buick ran out of gas.

Along Grove he drove faster and with more decision; at Ashby Avenue he turned left, toward the hills. Telegraph Avenue, College Avenue, Claremont Avenue, passed behind; forested hills rose beside the road; Ashby Avenue snaked back and forth and became Mountain Boulevard. Paul slackened speed, keeping a careful watch in the rear-view mirror. Behind came the Buick, lurching around the curves, lugging up the grades. Paul felt a quiver of doubt; his enemy must also be forming plans. He studied the rear-view mirror; the faceless shape told him nothing. Paul swung off to the left, up Tunnel Road, a meandering old byway leading nowhere in particular. A hundred yards behind came the inexorable Buick.

They wound back and forth, traversing the fir- and pine-wooded hillsides, with nowhere an inkling of the city so close at hand. Paul kept watch to the left, where, if memory served him, several steep little lanes dropped down from Skyline Boulevard. He passed the first of these, and looked back over his shoulder. It might have served his purpose —

although this purpose still was not exactly defined. Somehow, in some fashion, he hoped to drive up one of these side-streets, make a sudden U-turn, descend upon the Buick... Not a good plan, he decided gloomily. In the first place he'd be sure to wreck his own car. Secondly, there was no guarantee that he would destroy the driver of the Buick, unless he struck with such an impact as to endanger himself. He could leap free, of course... Ahead another narrow road opened into the Tunnel Road: Cornwall Way.

Paul swung smartly up this street, and under towering pines climbed toward the ridge. He passed a house, dark redwood and glass perched on stilts, then swung around a hair-pin curve. The Buick followed cautiously. Another house appeared ahead, cantilevered over a parking area. And here, lo and behold! A red and white Dodge convertible, festooned with glistening metal, awaiting Paul's pleasure.

He jerked to a halt a few yards up the road, ran back to the convertible. He looked up at the house, but a retaining wall barred the view. Paul sought across the resplendent dashboard: naturally, no key. At the bottom of the slope appeared the Buick, head-lamps peering cautiously up toward Paul.

Paul threw off the handbrake, set the gear-selector in neutral, ran behind the car, heaved. The Dodge moved, inched over to the road, rolled free. Paul ran forward, twisted the wheel, steered the convertible out into the road. It gathered speed; Paul sprang clear, ran back to his own car.

Downhill slid the red and white Dodge. The Buick paused in alarm, then pulled over to the side. Paul watched intently as the Dodge swerved first to the left, then to right, then hurtled off the pavement, struck a pine tree. The crash and crunch of rending metal echoed up the hill. Paul hissed through his teeth in annoyance. He looked up at the house. It was time to leave. He fled up the hill. Behind came the Buick, the infuriated vengeful Buick.

Paul raced up Cornwall, turned into Barham, came out on Skyline Boulevard. A vast panorama lay before him: the whole of San Francisco Bay, surrounded by twenty microscopically textured cities. Paul spared the vista no attention; he had remembered a trick of the road ahead. After making sure that the Buick still followed, he proceeded with new optimism.

He must time the operation carefully, with exactly the right distance between himself and the Buick. And there was the normal Skyline Boulevard traffic to be taken into account... Paul watched his rear-view mirror. No sign of the Buick, which was well. He must not be observed when he arrived at the turn-off... Here it was: a short-cut, no more than a rutted track over a hump of ridge, while Skyline Boulevard made a swing to the west. As Paul recalled, the short-cut returned to the road where the mountainside dropped steeply away. If he came down the dirt road at exactly the right instant, sideswiped the Buick, it would roll and tumble half a mile. There would be little damage to his own car.

A final glance in his rear-view mirror: no Buick. He swung up the dirt track, bumped over the ridge, turned back down toward the road. Fifty feet short, he stopped, poised carefully. The situation was perfect. The Buick, intent on the road, would never notice him. Paul waited. Seconds passed. A half-minute. Where was the Buick? He heard a vibration of motor, a whir of tires. He let his car slip forward, gather momentum. Here it came! The black bulging fenders, the crafty headlight! Black hood, white side-panels. Red searchlight. Paul frantically braked. His wheels locked, he slewed down the dirt track, out into the road. His bumper crumpled the polished rear fender.

Paul sat back on the seat, turned off the engine. Two uniformed patrolmen alighted from the car with significant deliberation.

Ten minutes later the patrol-car moved on. Paul followed circumspectly. A citation for reckless driving lay on the seat beside him. In due course he would be billed for damages to the fender. If the patrolmen had their way, Paul's license would be revoked. Look at that drop beside the road! Think what might have happened if Paul had hit them squarely! Paul bowed his head. A miscalculation, an error of judgment, which he regretted. While they were talking a bulge-fendered old Buick rumbled past and disappeared to the north.

Paul drove back in the direction he had come. The road was clear; he and the Buick had lost each other. The sun was setting into the Pacific; golden haze blurred San Francisco; Oakland and Berkeley were streaked with long dark shadows.

Paul descended into the twilight, returned to Berkeley. In a mood of depression he drove up Telegraph to the University campus. Observing the students on the sidewalks, in the restaurants, Paul felt grim and remote. He parked, went into one of the brightly-lit restaurants, ordered a sandwich and coffee.

He sat for a long time, considering the mess in which he found himself. Si Bethea need only telephone Neil Hubbard to plunge Paul into the hottest kind of water. Worse, Si might even kill Paul.

Paul examined the situation from every aspect. There were various remedies for his troubles, falling into three categories: retreat, evasion, attack. Under Category One, for example, he could appeal to the police for protection, thereby focusing attention upon the sideline to his Welfare work... Paul thought of Article 7: 'I have unalterable faith in myself, nothing else. There is no other entity or institution capable of inspiring faith. I trust only myself. I can never doubt the range of my own capabilities; if I doubt, I compromise my dynamic assault against Destiny.'

Category One was out.

Category Two: evasion. He could quit his job, take himself out of circulation for a while. Or he could submit to Si's demands and accept him as a partner — whereby the profits would be halved, the risks doubled. Si Bethea would indulge in drunken boasting; both he and Paul would be arrested, convicted and sent to San Quentin.

Category Two: out.

Category Three: attack — and suddenly Paul marveled that he could even have considered retreat. He felt a resurgence of energy. Objective: seek out, destroy the enemy. How?

Paul considered ways and means. The automobile as a weapon must be abandoned; he had exhausted its potentialities.

Other weapons existed, for instance the .30-.30 rifle his father had used years ago to slaughter deer. Paul nodded thoughtfully. The rifle, a vantage-point, patience. A careful squeeze of the finger — and the difficulties represented by Si Bethea would dissipate.

The first step was to secure the rifle. It lay on a shelf in the closet of his old room, together with his father's hunting jacket. All during childhood Paul had wondered about the gun, the jacket, the mounted trophies. Why had his father not taken them after the divorce? One day his mother made a careful explanation: Paul's father was a very selfish man; he had deprived Lillian Gunther of spiritual association and many other benefits; in presenting an opal brooch to a girl friend he had wrongfully disposed of a treasured heirloom. It was only fair and right that certain of *his* cherished possessions should be sequestered. Lillian Gunther would relinquish the gun, the jacket and the trophies when the heirloom had been restored. Apparently this was not feasible; the trophies hung on the wall.

Paul left the restaurant, walked to a sporting-goods store, bought a box of cartridges.

He returned to his car, drove up Bancroft Way, crossed north over the campus, returned down the hill to Halcyon Way and the Yvanette Arms.

He looked up the front of the building. A strip of lighted windows on the third floor informed him that his mother was home. Paul drove off in annoyance. His mother, in almost constant attendance at concerts, lectures, study groups, meetings of her literary association, had chosen this particular evening for idleness.

Driving without destination, Paul found himself back down on San Pablo Avenue. Now where? West Oakland? Not to the house on Corinth Street. Not tonight at any rate...What of his briefcase, was it safe in the cottage? It contained, in addition to various applications, forms, vouchers and reports, the black leatherette notebook.

It would be wise, thought Paul, to remove this briefcase to premises more secure from visitors. Perhaps tomorrow, after he had secured the gun... In this connection he must learn if his mother were planning to leave the apartment during the evening. Paul pulled into a service station, telephoned from the booth. His mother's voice responded: "Lillian Gunther speaking."

"This is Garnett, Mother."

"Garnett! How nice of you to call! Where are you?"

"Downtown. I'm working late."

"On Saturday evening? Odd!"

"Yes, it's unusual. Things have been piling up on us. I thought perhaps if we got done at a reasonable hour I might drop by. That is, if you plan to be home."

"I'd love to see you, Garry! We haven't had a chat for simply ages."

"Then you're not going out?"

"I'm just too tired tonight, even though it's Bridge Club. I thought I'd spend a nice evening at home."

"Excuse me, Mother, I'll ask Mr. Perkins how late we'll be." Paul put his hand over the mouthpiece, waited ten or twenty seconds. He spoke again in a doleful voice, "Confound everything, it looks as if I'll be here until midnight. Perkins has just come in with an armload of reports and we'll have to summarize them before we leave."

"Oh Garry! I'm so sorry! When will I see you, dear? Will you come for dinner tomorrow?"

"Well, I've got a date, Mother. But early next week — say Tuesday or Wednesday — I'll drop by."

"Yes, Garnett, you must. I see so little of you since you've gone out on your own. You don't know how I worry about you."

"I'm perfectly well, Mother. Absolutely A-1. How've you been?"

"Oh, you know me, I always seem to have my little ailments. Nothing serious, or so we hope. Dr. Stannage wants me to lose five pounds, and he's worked out a diet for me. He's such a wonderful man."

"Well, you take care of yourself, Mother, and I'll see you in two or three days."

"Goodnight, Garry dear, I'm so glad you called."

"Goodnight, Mother."

Paul returned to the sidewalk. His mother might be expected to stay up until ten-thirty. Then she'd make herself a cup of Ovaltine, take it to bed with her.

He stood looking up and down the street. Over the sidewalk, out to the limit of vision, colored tubes flickered, shone, and vibrated: vermilion, green, blue. Behind hung the luminous night sky. Automobiles, emerging from a molten river, slid past with a rush of air, a sigh of tires, a sidewise glare of headlights. Everywhere motion, light, the feel of time and space. The moment held an enormous significance, which poised just beyond the brink of Paul's understanding. Near at hand stood Destiny, sharing Paul's perceptions of color, twinkle, glow and motion, perhaps feeling the same wry melancholy... Paul swung his arms energetically. The mood was unreal. It diminished the urgency of his problem. Very well then. At eleven his mother would be asleep. At midnight he could enter the apartment, secure the rifle and leave.

Meanwhile? Four hours. He toyed with the idea of calling Barbara, rejected it. He went into a bar for a bottle of beer, but the television drove him out. He sat in his car a few minutes, then, without any particular destination in mind, set off down San Pablo. Perhaps a bit of reconnaissance might be in order...

Si told George Shaw, "I go in my house, I wonder what that man like to do next. He's out to get me, I know that, and I know I better jump lively."

"What about the police?" Shaw asked gently. "Did you forget all about us?"

Si snorted. "What good the police do me? Suppose I say, 'Look here, Mr. Policeman, a man tryin' to bump me off. I want you to arrest that man' — what he say? 'Mr. Si, I sure sorry to see you drinkin' cheap booze. You go home or I run you in.' And I say, 'Mr. Policeman, I ain't foolin'. That man run me down with my own Buick. Just this afternoon he let fly a big Dodge automobile. Please, Mr. Policeman, arrest that man before he do damage!' He say, 'Mr. Si, get lost.' What do I do?" Si held out his hands, pale palms turned upwards.

"You knew he was Mr. Big," said Shaw. "How come you didn't report it?"

"Wouldn't do no good."

Shaw nodded grimly. "Because once you talked to the police, that was the end of the racket. And you wanted in... But let's hear the rest of it."

Si continued in an injured voice. "Like I say, I wanta know what he up to. For sure he ain't gonna quit, just like that. Vinnie, she and Gally and Ainsworth, they gone to the show. I put up the automobile, I go in the front room by the window. I think sure as sure, that man come by the house. I sit there smokin' my cigar and pretty soon here he comes. He cruises by slow, I see him lookin' all around. I got my Buick in the shed, he can't see nothin'. He don't know where I am. As soon as he come past, I run out, jump in my car. I go out after him." Si paused, frowned at his cigar, struck a match, set fire to the end. Shaw watched without comment.

Si said, "I go after him. He drive here, he drive there. Pretty soon he go up into Berkeley. He stops beside a big apartment house. I stop too, but he don't see me..."

Paul drove south on San Pablo, toward the bright node of Central Oakland. Never had time moved so slow. What a relief to be finished with the whole business: to abandon the whole mess, quit his job, move back to Berkeley... He swung right into West Oakland, drove aimlessly through streets which at one time he had thought picturesque. He turned into Seventh Street with its markets and bars and juke-joints. There: Samphire's Bar-B-Q Hut. Si Bethea's hang-out. Paul slowed to a crawl, looked along the line of parked cars. No bulge-fendered Buick... Paul turned into Corinth, approached his cottage. He wondered about Gally, without any real interest. Five hundred and fifty dollars she'd cost him. Not that he worried about the money; there was always more coming in. Easy money charmed from nowhere by his ingenuity: he'd relinquish that money to no one! Paul's melancholy gave way to anger and resentment. Si Bethea had been warned. The issue was joined.

But there was no advantage in rashness. Si was looking for him, he was looking for Si. No telling where Si had taken himself, what he was planning... Paul slowed almost to a halt in front of the address on Corinth Street. He peered along the walk leading to his cottage; it was pitch-dark, the cottage showed no lights. The briefcase no doubt was secure. The black notebook? Presumably safe. Tomorrow he'd come for it.

He turned down Lily Street, approached Van Buren Avenue. There: the old house on the corner, which Gally had wanted him to buy. The weathered siding shone pallid in the light from the street-lamp, the house looked more forbidding than ever... He rounded the corner, passed the citadel of his enemy. No sign of the Buick. The windows were dark. Where was everybody? Paul felt a freakish impulse to halt, to go into the house, to wander the solitary rooms.

Paul drove on. The house seemed to stare after him. A chill coursed along Paul's spine. Boredom be damned, thought Paul, let's get the hell out of here. He twisted the steering-wheel, swung around the corner, stepped down hard on the gas-pedal.

To such effect that when Si lumbered to the shed, started the Buick with a snarl of starter and thump of bearings, roared out into Van Buren Avenue, Paul's convertible had reached San Pablo Avenue and was gone.

Si cursed and muttered. "That man he got sumpin' up his sleeve. That's all right, ol' Si he got a sleeve too."

He pulled over to the curb, sat thinking. "He gotta sleep somewhere. He ain't gonna come back to Corinth Street. Not tonight. Maybe he go to a motel. Maybe..." Si took a piece of paper from his pocket, the index from Paul's black notebook. In the sallow light of a street lamp he reverently read down the list of names, sucked in his breath. "Money. Easy money! And he try to collect from me! That man he just don't have sense!"

Si turned the page over, contemplated the address:

> G. Paul Gunther
> Yvanette Arms, Apt. 303
> 600 Halcyon Way
> ROsewood 4-9516

"Maybe, just maybe," said Si.

He climbed from the car, strode across the street to the service station. Outside the telephone booth he reached in his pocket, brought up a handful of change, selected a dime. Then he went into the booth, dialed RO4-9516.

A woman responded at the third ring, speaking in what Si thought of as a 'prissy-pants' voice. "Hello?"

"Hello," said Si. "I like to talk to Mr. Paul Gunther."

"Paul? But he doesn't live here now. I'm very sorry."

"Yeah," rumbled Si. "That's too bad."

"Is there any message? I'm his mother and I see him once or twice a week."

"No," said Si. "No message. Just tell him Mr. Big called."

" 'Mr. Big'?" The voice was puzzled and uncertain.

"That's right, ma'am, Mr. Big."

"Very well, I'll tell him. But I don't know when I'll be seeing him."

"That's okay, ma'am. Any time do good enough."

Si returned to his car, sat clutching the steering-wheel with both hands. Man need a place to sleep. Where else he go but his mother's house? No harm taking a look. Might just catch that man and give him a good fixing. Like he give me. Three, four months in the hospital. And he trying the same thing again. But this time we both in the game... Gotta watch for them cops, thought Si. They don't give a black man no chance. Play it cool, slow easy—hit *hard*! Like a big horse kicking. That thump hurt when it hit. Do it careful, but do it good... Si ground his car into life, listened half-critically, half-affectionately, to the sounds from under the hood. When he was Mr. Big for real he'd junk this heap, get a real car, something shiny and new. He'd get two, three good suits, good hat, good shoes. People look after him, they say, who that big man? And other people say, don't you know? Where you been? That's Si Bethea, big gambling man, real big-shot... Nobody in his way but that smart young snot supposed to be the Welfare Man. Si chuckled sardonically. He really welfare me. Put me in the hospital. He really welfare Gally. Put a baby up her belly. He really welfare all them people, take their money... That man got to sleep somewhere: where he go? A motel? Not when his mother got a good home. Better just drive over to Berkeley, can't take chances missing out.

Si pulled out into the street, turned north at San Pablo and drove toward Berkeley.

Chapter XIII

Paul Gunther

Paul's plans were simple. He would secure the gun, return to West Oakland, find a suitable vantage point, and wait. When Si appeared, Paul would shoot him. Then he would drive across the Richmond-San Rafael bridge and drop the gun into the bay. The program was uncomplicated and should work out very well. If he were asked questions, he need only state that he had been asleep in the cottage. Who could prove differently? Or he might return to his mother's apartment. In the morning she would be surprised to see him; Paul would display an equal surprise: "Good heavens, Mother, we talked five minutes last night when I came in." His mother would pretend to remember, and the fictitious visit would become fact.

Paul sat through a program at one of the small theaters near the campus, then headed for his mother's apartment. From bygone habit he approached along Mariposa, parked before rounding the corner. Si Bethea, across from Yvanette Arms in the deep shade of a sidewalk oak, almost missed him. He saw a figure in gray slacks and dark coat quietly appear, look up at the windows of the third floor, which now were dark. As Paul entered the garden court, realization came to Si. He lurched to the sidewalk, ran across the street. If he could get his hands on the man, just get close... He was too late. He entered the courtyard just as the front door closed on Paul.

Through the plate-glass, Si watched Paul cross the red-tiled foyer, start up the stairs with the ease of old habit.

Si clenched his fist, shook it slowly. He returned to the Buick, looking up over his shoulder as he crossed the street. When he reached his car he still stood looking... Mighty strange, thought Si. Don't the man turn on the lights? Maybe he don't need no lights, maybe he sees in the dark. "I wait just a while," muttered Si. "I see what he tryin' to do..."

Paul mounted the stairs. At the even rhythm of his steps he thought of his Adversary. The march of Destiny! Paul thrust the idea roughly aside. Not the march of Destiny. Merely my feet on the stairs! I am master of this situation! ... He reached the third floor in a mood so exalted as almost to override caution. But the sight of the familiar door, the thought of his mother in the dark rooms behind, gave him pause. He resumed his stealth.

First: unscrew the light in the hall, so that no shaft of light should precede him into the apartment. Then key in the lock, gently, and gently turn. Ease open the door with the weight of his shoulder. Step into the entry, close the—he froze. From the bedroom came a sound alarmingly loud. A cough. Another cough. The creak of bed-springs.

His mother was not yet asleep.

Paul backed out of the apartment, eased the door shut. He resisted the impulse to swear; to do so would merely delight the Foe.

Very well then. There was no hurry. He would wait another hour.

Descending to the foyer, he pushed open the heavy glass door, went out into the night. Through the courtyard he wandered, listening to the fountain playing into the fish-pond, inhaling the scent of the deodars. A pair of girls passed along Halcyon Way, laughing and talking. Paul sauntered to the gate, looked after them. Girls... He returned to the garden, seated himself on a stone bench. An hour to wait. No great hardship. Chances were that Si still caroused at Samphire's. There'd be ample time to waylay him as he staggered home... Paul frowned. Si might be out prowling in his Buick. Si might be near or far.

Si was near. Si came through the shadows. In one hand he carried a loop of thin wire, tied in a loose overhand knot. He crept over a bed of primula, lurked behind a six-foot cylinder of privet. He approached the stone bench from the rear. Now he stood up, holding the garrote outstretched. Paul, lazing on the bench, felt the presence; he threw a startled look over his shoulder, gasped, squealed, fell back off the bench. Si lunged; the wire loop missed. Si lumbered around the bench. Paul, trying to gain his feet, fell flat, rolled to the side. Si's foot struck his leg; Si gave a hoarse grunt, reached forward. Scratching and clawing the gravel, Paul lunged blindly into Si, who toppled back into the stone bench.

Paul ran for the door to the apartment. He fumbled his keys — a nightmare situation! Select the key, thrust it home, while Si came lurching up the path. He opened the door, jumped inside, slammed the door. A body darkened the glass, eyes looked in at him, glaring red. Paul backed away, panting, furiously angry. Taken by surprise, ambushed! Almost killed! Two could play that game! A weapon, a weapon. In the garage? What kind of weapon could be found in the garage? Tire-iron, jack-handle, lug-wrench...

Si was gone; the glass was clear. Paul descended three steps, pushed open the door leading to the garage. He flipped up the light. Five cars occupied their allotted niches: sleek, shiny, waxed.

Paul went to the cupboard, flung wide the doors. No weapon. A few cans of paint, some miscellaneous bottles, a stack of old magazines. He must improvise. Everywhere in the world people made lethal devices from unlikely bits and pieces. For instance, Si's garrote... Paul knew what he would do.

He secured a quart mayonnaise jar, one with the lid intact. On a ledge he found a beer-can opener, which might suffice for the purpose he had in mind. He went to the nearest car, a fancy hardtop, bent under the rear deck, tried to puncture the gas tank with the beer-can opener. He fumbled, scraped; nothing happened. He wedged the point under a strap, levered. The point cut metal; gasoline jetted forth. Paul filled the quart jar, backed away. Gasoline spread across the floor, filling the air with pungency.

Paul took the jar of gasoline to the bench, punched a hole in the cap. Into this hole he inserted a strip of rag, screwed the cap back upon the jar. The wick floated in the gasoline.

Paul went to the door which led into the street. It was secured against entry by a snap-latch. He hesitated. What if Si stood outside? He'd throw the un-fired Molotov Cocktail into Si's face, run back through the foyer, out the front door, and away. Behind him fifteen gallons of gasoline made a black puddle; the fumes permeated his brain. He felt dizzy and gay. He flung open the door — to reveal dark emptiness. No Si. Paul stepped out upon the sidewalk, ran with shadow-like strides up Mariposa Street to the corner. Here he paused, peered around the angle of the building.

He saw Si, a shape standing near the gate, peering into the court. As he watched, Si moved back and looked up toward his mother's apartment. Paul chuckled softly. Pretty soon now, Si, pretty soon...

A middle-aged couple came walking up Halcyon Way, bickering in tired voices. Si slunk across the street, disappeared into the shadows. The couple turned into the Yvanette Garden Court. The door opened, shut. Once more there was silence.

Across the street shadows were deep under the oak trees. Paul heard the click and thud of an automobile door. He strained his eyes, trying to separate the bulks and shapes. Peering, squinting, he saw that Si now sat almost invisible in the front seat of his car.

Paul deliberated. He could not cross the street without being noticed. Unless he went entirely around the block, approached Si from the rear... He turned, ran fleetly back down Mariposa Street.

Si leaned forward, pointed a stubby finger at George Shaw. "Now I'm gonna tell you something maybe you won't believe. Here I am sittin' at home. I think, I just drive out to Berkeley, talk to that man's mother. Maybe she put some sense into him — because if he don't leave me alone I know he gonna get hurt." Si shook his head dourly. "That's something I don't like. I just mooch along, mind my own business, so long as folks leave me be. They push me too hard — watch out! That's what I wanta tell his mother.

"Anyway I gets in my car and I drives out to Berkeley. I parks down the street from the apartment house, and here comes Paul. He say to me mad-like, 'What you want out here?' Just like that.

"I say, 'Boy, I gonna talk to your mother. Maybe she lick some sense into you.'

"He say, 'She don't want to talk to you. She pretty fussy who she talk to. You better just fly on back where you come from. We don't want people like you around here.'

"I say, 'Don't push me, white boy. I gonna talk to your mother, you like it or not.'

"And he say, 'You are, hey? That right now.'

"I say, 'That sure is right. I gonna talk to your mother.'

"Then he say, 'You wait just a few minutes, I see if she's in bed. You go back to your car, I come down and tell you what's what.'

"I say, 'Okay, that suits me. Just so long as I get to talk to the woman, that's all I want.'

"I got my automobile parked a block up the street. I see this Pontiac and I think, I just sit here awhile. So I sit and I sit. I wonder, just what that man up to? I don't see him come out. I start gettin' fidgety. I know that man real mean. I don't trust him worth a cent. Good thing for me. I look in the rear-view mirror, I see a man come down the sidewalk behind me. I don't think much about it. But this man actin' awful funny. He come up quiet and slow. Then he light a match. I think, that's all right, man fix himself a cigarette or a cigar. Then a big flame shoots up; it's Paul holdin' a bottle! He fling this big bottle, and I think, oh my lawd, Si, your time has come. I just dive for the door. I busts it open, I fall out in the street. The bottle flies through the window. Whoom! Big splash of fire, like the world blowin' up! If I don't see through that rear-view mirror, I ain't here now talkin' to you. I just barely escape, by the skin of the britches.

"Paul, he don't know I slip out. He can't see with all that fire flashin' around. He runs across the street like he's really proud. Me, I kinda crawl out of the way. I tell you, I never been so mad in my born days. Can't hardly see straight. I set out after Paul. If I catch him, then I really gonna fix him.

"I run around the corner, I see him gettin' in his car. Now he sees me. For a minute he stares like he see a ghost, like he can't believe it's me. Then he starts up the car, cuts off down the hill. I run back to my old Buick. Lot of people out watchin' the Pontiac. One man there real excited, he jumpin' up and down hollerin', 'Why for they burn my car?'

"I get in my automobile, I take after Paul. I see him turnin' the corner down Fulton Street. He gets mixed in traffic at University Avenue, and I pull up behind him." Si shook his head slowly. "Ain't too smart.

If I stay back maybe I get a chance at him. Right away he sees me. He knows me and the ol' Buick there behind him..."

Paul's skin felt clammy; his fingers twitched and shivered on the steering-wheel. Behind him drove a dark creature, malignant, indestructible. As relentless as — the words froze in Paul's mind, a new and oddly dreadful idea occurring to him.

Paul took a deep gasp of air, sat straight in the seat. No. The car behind was driven by Si Bethea. And yet on the other hand, if the Creed were truth...

He was away, driving as rapidly as he dared. The Buick became lost among the swarm of head-lights. Paul turned left, up toward Telegraph Avenue. Behind him turned another car, unidentifiable. At Telegraph, Paul turned right toward Oakland. The car turned after him. He no longer had any doubt. Si was on his track.

Paul set his teeth. This is the challenge. The great challenge. I'll meet it, I'll win.

Paul accelerated, passed the traffic signal at Ashby, just as the light turned yellow.

Red light glared at the Buick. Si ignored the signal, drove through without slackening speed. Paul stared back in wonder. Somehow this seemed the most flagrant act of all! There were basic rules by which the Game of Life was played; Si refused to heed them.

"A man like that shouldn't be allowed to drive," muttered Paul.

How to lose him? Drive him out of gas? Outspeed him on the freeway? Or — a really beautiful idea came to Paul. Beautiful and simple. It depended on Barbara Tavistock.

She'd be home, she'd told him so Thursday. She'd be awake; Barbara detested going to bed early. Would she let him take her car? That remained to be seen.

Paul drove along Highland Avenue, through the Piedmont shopping district, into the area of twisting hillside roads, along Flores Way. Behind came Si Bethea. Paul turned into the Tavistock driveway. He frowned at the sight of an old green Ford sedan. Jim Connor. What was he doing here? Paul jerked on brakes, ran up to the front door. Over his shoulder he saw that Si had halted out in the street.

Barbara opened the door. Never had Paul seen anyone so beautiful. At once cool and warm, near and remote...

"Hello Paul."

"Can I come in?"

Barbara silently stood aside. From the living room came the sound of music, a flicker of flames. Jim Connor came out into the hall, looked Paul over with only the faintest curiosity. Tonight Connor was as nothing: a figure in the background, unimportant, colorless. Life consisted of Paul and Destiny, who now wore the guise of Si Bethea.

Barbara said with faintly bitter humor, "You seem excited, Paul."

"Excited?" Paul evaluated himself. "I don't think so."

Barbara looked at him skeptically. Connor listlessly picked up *Town & Country* from an old teak tabouret.

There was silence. Jim Connor put down the magazine, made a dispassionate inspection of Paul. Barbara spoke in a voice falsely bright. "Would you like a cup of coffee, Paul?"

"I'd like some coffee," said Paul courteously.

"Let's go into the living room," said Barbara. "It's nice by the fire."

Paul took a seat on the sofa, Connor lowered himself into a chair. Barbara went out into the kitchen for coffee.

"What brings you out this way?" asked Connor.

Paul considered. "It's a long story... Essentially, the instinct of self-preservation." He turned to look at Connor. "What brings you out?"

"One thing and another. Animal high spirits. Free coffee."

Paul rose to his feet. "I think I'll go see how the coffee's coming." He went out into the kitchen. Barbara looked up, then became absorbed in filling the coffee-maker.

Paul leaned casually against a wall. "For some reason or another things haven't worked out too well with us."

Barbara made a nervously flippant gesture. "It happens all the time."

"I don't suppose you want to try again?"

"No."

"You're probably sensible," said Paul. "Incidentally, I've become involved in a minor difficulty. I wonder if you could help me out."

Barbara stared at him. "What kind of difficulty?"

Paul laughed. "Nothing too serious. A man wants to kill me. In fact, he's looking for me right now."

Barbara sought to keep her voice cool and impersonal. "If I were you, I'd go to the police."

"Heavens no," said Paul. "They'd spoil everything."

Barbara turned back to the coffee-maker. "I'm afraid I don't understand any of this."

"It's perfectly simple," said Paul. "He's after me, I'm after him. Like a game of musical chairs. One of us gets left out in the cold."

Barbara studied him in fascination. "Do you mean that you're planning to kill this man?"

"That's a harsh way of putting it," said Paul.

Barbara picked up the tray. "I don't care to be involved in anything like that. You'd better try another of your girl friends."

Paul raised his eyebrows sardonically. "But I merely want to borrow your car for an hour or two."

"Tonight? Right now?"

"Yes."

Barbara shook her head. "I wouldn't think of it."

"Very well," said Paul without resentment. "It's not important. Do you know Jeff Pettigrew's home address?"

"Not offhand. I've got it written down somewhere. I seriously doubt if he'll lend you his car."

Paul laughed. "This is a business matter."

"I'll see if I can find it."

Paul took the coffee tray; they returned to the living room. Barbara poured coffee, then went to find Jeff Pettigrew's address.

Connor picked up a magazine; Paul walked quietly to the front window, stood in the shadow of the drapes, looked out across the lawn.

Barbara came in from the hall. "Where… Oh. There you are."

Paul returned to the fireplace. He put down his coffee cup, took the address. "Thank you very much. And now, I think I'll be leaving. May I use the back door?"

Barbara giggled nervously. "If that's what you want." She conducted him back through the kitchen, out upon the service porch. Paul opened the door a crack, looked out. He turned to Barbara, said, "Goodnight, and thank you," then stepped out into the dark.

Barbara closed and bolted the door, turned to find Jim Connor behind her. "Oh... You startled me."

"I wanted to make sure you weren't having trouble."

"Oh no," said Barbara distantly. "Nothing like that."

They returned to the living room. Barbara stirred up the fire. Connor wandered restlessly back and forth. "Maybe I'll be going too."

"No, Jimmy. Don't go yet. Mother and Daddy will be back any minute. And I feel all spooky."

"He's jumped the rails," said Connor. "Just how and why I don't know. But something very strange is going on."

Barbara nodded gloomily. "If I could understand him I'd feel much less uncomfortable... But he's acting so oddly."

She went to the front window, looked out, gave a small stifled cry.

Connor crossed the room. "What's the matter?"

"I thought I saw someone out there."

"Gunther?"

"No... Not Paul. Somebody else, much bigger than Paul."

Connor looked from the window. "There's nobody there now..."

Paul felt his way through the darkness to the side fence, where he stopped under a laurel tree to listen. No sound. He looked through the leaves along the street. It was dimly lit by a street-lamp at the corner where Mara Road intersected Flores Way. A few dark parked cars were visible, none familiar.

Paul climbed the fence, dropped into Mara Road. Twenty minutes walk took him into the center of Piedmont, where he flagged a taxi. "600 Halcyon Way in Berkeley," he told the driver.

The taxi stopped in front of the Yvanette Arms. Paul made a careful survey of the scene. The burned car had been towed away. His mother's windows were dark. There was no sign of the Buick.

He stepped out into the street, paid off the driver. The taxi drove off. He was alone. The air was chill, smoky with fog; the streets were silent. Paul warily walked through the courtyard.

The fountain splashed peacefully; there was a pleasant odor of mold, geraniums, violets.

Paul let himself into the building, walked up the stairs to his mother's apartment.

Carefully he opened the door. The entry hall was dark, warm, silent. He stepped inside, closed the door.

He waited while his eyes became accustomed to the dim light. From his mother's bedroom through the half-open door, he seemed to hear the sound of her breathing.

With velvety steps he went along the carpet of the hall, feeling with his hands on the wall. He came to the door into his old bedroom. He groped for the knob, eased the door open, listened. Silence. Paul entered the room, closed the door. Without turning on the light he crossed the familiar distance to the wardrobe. He found the door, slid it back with a faint rustle of rolling wheels. Into his face came the smell of long-unused clothes, empty card-board boxes, sachet, a whiff of moth-balls. Paul drew back, his heart thumping. What if by some mad chance Si stood here in the wardrobe, an enormous shape... Nonsense. Si waited on Flores Way in his great bloated Buick.

Paul reached forward, felt behind the miscellaneous odds and ends. There, on the upper shelf, wrapped in a canvas hunting jacket, the gun.

Working carefully, he drew the gun loose, brought it out of the closet. With no sound he laid it on the barely-seen bed, re-arranged the upper shelf, closed the wardrobe doors. The only sound was the faint click and whir of the overhead wheels.

Paul stood in the dark, thrilling to a sense of power. The feeling was almost hypnotic; he might have stayed ten seconds, a minute, three minutes. Then he moved, with a nervous jerk. He picked up the gun, went to the door. Pressure on the knob, the controlled turning, the slow opening of the door. He went out into the hall. As he passed his mother's bedroom he heard her twist over in bed. She muttered uneasily, called something in a plaintive voice, then sighed, and returned to sleep.

Paul went to the outer door. He slipped quickly through and was gone.

Down in the street he inspected his prize. Wrapped in the hunting jacket, it might be anything.

He walked up to Euclid Avenue, found a taxi at the stand. He gave the address of the Tavistock house in Piedmont. Before alighting he had the driver take him the length of Flores Way, around the corner, back up Mara.

There was no sign of Si or the Buick. The streets were empty of threat. Paul's car was still parked in the Tavistock driveway; Si apparently had decided that here was where Paul would spend the night.

Paul paid off the driver, took the gun to his car. The Tavistock house was dark and withdrawn. Paul gave it no consideration. Never would he come here again. The name 'Barbara', once a perfume in his mind, now rasped in his ears. And Connor, once a challenge to Paul's uniqueness and integrity, seemed merely another rather vacuous face... Paul touched the gun on the seat beside him, hefted the box of shells. Tomorrow, tomorrow...

Chapter XIV

Mr. Big

Paul slept in his car, behind a lumber warehouse. Early sunlight awoke him. He stretched the cramps from his muscles, rubbed the dry skin of his face. Sunday morning. But no coffee, no bacon and eggs, no Sunday newspaper.

He examined the rifle without interest. In the bright sunlight the situation he found himself in seemed absurd. Impatiently Paul started his car, headed for Corinth Street. Halfway, he pulled to the curb, loaded the rifle, then continued.

Corinth Street had not yet awakened when he arrived. He parked, wrapped the gun in the hunting jacket, marched briskly back along the walk to his cottage. He put his key in the lock, flung open the door.

He stood stock-still. The room seemed warm, humid, as if from a human presence. He called, "Gally?"

No reply.

Slowly Paul advanced. A cool draft flew against his cheek. He looked into the bedroom. The bed was rumpled, the window was open. Paul put his hand under the coverlets. Warmth. Who had slept in his bed? And fled through the window at the sound of a key?

Somberly Paul bathed and shaved. Then he cooked himself breakfast.

Si told George Shaw, "I figger he be comin' back to that little house on Corinth Street. All his fixin's there; he got to come back. I call Ainsworth, I told him, 'You get the key off of Gally, you go in that house, don't you leave till the man come down the walk. That's when you leave — fast. You come tell me, then I take care of things.' So Ainsworth goes and next thing I know he comes runnin' back. Still pretty early in the morning.

"I say, 'Boy, what I tell you? You get back up that house, don't you stir till the man come home.'

"Ainsworth get mad at me. He cry out, 'He already come home! Big as life, twice as natural.'

"I tell him, 'You go back up there, watch things till I get a chance to come up personal.'

"Ainsworth say, 'I ain't goin' back there. That man carry a big gun.'

"I tell Ainsworth, just go up and do like I explain.

"After awhile I set out. I ain't scared, but I ain't gonna let that man line up no gun-barrel on me. First thing I talk to Henry Samphire. I leave him my Buick, I take his truck. I drive along Corinth Street and park where I can see what's goin' on. Ainsworth he settin' on a porch across the street like he own the whole district.

"I call him over, tell him to go home. Pretty soon here comes the Welfare Man. He's got a package, and the way he carry it, it got some weight. I duck down, he don't see me. He starts up his automobile. I wait till he turn the corner; that way he don't know I'm after him.

"He don't go far. He drives by my house and I see him lookin' it over, up and down. I glad I ain't sittin' in the front window, him with that big gun. He drives around the corner, down to San Pablo. He stops by the real estate office. McAteel Realty, that's the place. After awhile he comes out and climbs in his car. He starts up and I start up, but I can't follow him. He sure gone fast.

"I go back to the McAteel Realty. Girl in front office speak to me real polite. 'Yes sir? What you like me to do for you?'

" 'Friend of mine just come in,' I tell her. 'Welfare man, maybe you know him.'

" 'Oh yes,' she say, 'I sure do. That's Mr. Paul Gunther, friend of Mr. Pettigrew.'

"I act like I'm kinda surprised. 'What Gunther want in here?'

"The girl gets a little huffy. 'We ain't allowed to talk about folks' business. You lookin' for a house?'

"I tell her yes, I like a big house, clean, nice respectable neighborhood.

"She say, 'You better talk to Mr. Pettigrew; he in charge of all that nice stuff.' She call into her telephone, 'Oh, Mr. Pettigrew, gentleman here lookin' for a house.'

"I go in to see this Mr. Pettigrew. Big blond-head man. I say, 'Happen to see my friend Mr. Paul Gunther just come out. What's he doin' around here?'

"Blond-head man look me up, look me down. He say, 'What you want to know for?'

"I say, 'Mr. Gunther, he's a good friend of yours?'

"He say, 'Oh, nothing special.'

"I say, 'How'd you like to see that man catch a good bust in the nose?'

"He laugh and say, 'Once or twice I feel like it myself.'

"I tell him, 'That's what I got in mind.'

"He look around careful. He say, 'You look like a man who can keep his mouth shut.'

"I say, 'I sure can.'

"The blond-head man spill the beans. He tell me that Mr. Gunther got the key for this old house up on Lily Street. He can't figure why. I know but I ain't lettin' on. I say I might just be interested in buyin' this house, and I ask if he got extra keys.

"He hems and haws. He don't like it too much, but he gives me the keys. 'Strickly business proposition,' he says. 'Remember I told you nothing.'

" 'Correct,' I say. 'You ain't told me nothing, I ain't heard nothing.'

" 'Correct,' he say, and hand over the keys.

"I go on out. I figger now I know what I do. That Paul, he out gunnin' for me, with a real gun. I figger I just go in this house, I wait till Paul comes; I catch him, bust up his gun, give him a good beatin'. I go take a look at that house, real careful-like. I see Paul there already, sittin' by the upstairs window. I look at that door, around the side of the house. Once it get dark, I can make it to that door and he won't see me."

Chapter XV

The Final Adversary

Paul left the realty office and stood for a moment in the sunlight. The warmth soothed him, he felt languid and lax. It was a calm still day; a smoky membrane sheathed the sky, tinging the sunlight with amber. Paul started slowly back toward his car, thinking wistfully of the old serene times. Would things ever be the same again? He felt sick of the whole business. There were other ways to make money... He burned with sudden indignation. Why must he abandon the enterprise he had conceived and founded? Here was the basic issue! He was only fighting for his rights!... Paul got into his car. He searched the street. No Buick in sight. This might mean much or little.

He swung out into the traffic, accelerated swiftly, beat a traffic light, and noted that no car had followed him through. He turned down a side-street, turned again. There was definitely no one on his tail.

He ate lunch at a drive-in. Ahead of him lay the crisis. Another few hours should bring this nightmare weekend to a close... By a circuitous route he drove toward the old house on Lily Street, parked two blocks away, on Adair Street. He took the long package from the front seat, a flashlight from the glove-compartment, then locked the car. No telling how long he'd be gone.

He walked with nervous strides toward Lily Street, conscious of a stealth which he felt must be apparent to the people he met on the way. But no one appeared to notice him, no one turned to look after him as he passed.

He approached the corner of Van Buren Avenue, and the ramshackle old house. He paused, glanced up and down the sidewalk, then ran quickly up the steps. He put the key in the lock, opened the door, made a quick entry. He closed the door carefully, watching through the diminishing crack. He had aroused no notice whatever.

He shut the door finally and definitely. He was alone in the house, a creature separated from the rest of humanity. He waited while his eyes adjusted to the dimness, his ears to the silence... He stood on blue- and white-checked linoleum in an entry hall. The walls showed a faded gold-striped wall-paper; ahead of him stairs rose to the second floor. The air smelled of dust, sour varnish, mouldering newspaper.

Paul advanced to the foot of the stairs. A far door opened into the dismal kitchen. On the right was the dining room, with a parquetry floor, floral wall-paper, a broken overhead light-fixture; on the left was the living room, strewn with old newspapers. Paul paused to examine the living room from various angles. He crossed to the window, newspapers rustling beneath his feet. Across the street the Bethea house lay full in view. A shadow seemed to pass through the Bethea front room.

Paul drew back quickly. Standing back out of sight he peered intently, but saw nothing. He mounted the stairs to the second floor. The house was as fragile and resonant as an old guitar; the shuffle of his footsteps returned from everywhere.

He went directly to the corner bedroom. There was a broken-down bed in one corner, a half-dozen bundles of newspapers in another.

Paul sidled to the window. The situation could not have been improved. Not only did this vantage-point overlook the Bethea front yard, but also commanded the length of Van Buren Avenue. He loosened the hasp at the window, lifted. The window rose four inches with a scrape and a groan... Paul jerked back, peered gingerly across at the Bethea front room. Another flicker of motion? Or his imagination?... Standing back from the window Paul unwrapped the rifle, leaned it against the wall. He brought three bundles of newspapers across the room, arranged a seat for himself, laid the flashlight on the floor. Now there was nothing to do but wait.

Time passed: half an hour, an hour. Rather a pleasant period. The room was warm, the odor of the old house antique and mysterious.

Paul sat alert, yet half-dreaming; he looked up at the sky, high and remote. A long shoal of herring-bone cloud glimmered in the sunlight. Paul felt unaccountably melancholy. He turned his attention back to the street.

At three o'clock Gally marched out of the front door — rather sullenly, Paul thought — and walked up Van Buren Avenue toward Ninth. Paul aimed the gun at a spot between her shoulder-blades. The act was devoid of rancor, no more than an exercise... Gally dwindled down Van Buren Avenue, turned the corner, disappeared.

Other pedestrians appeared, passed below, vanished. There was no sign of Si. Paul pulled the broken old bed across the room, made himself more comfortable. Impatience was useless. Sooner or later Si would pass in front of his rifle sights, and that one instant would be enough.

Afternoon became evening. The sunlight darkened through the yellows, golds and tawny golds, the sky became pearl and citron. There was the glitter of a star or two.

The street-lights came on. Paul watched intently. Now was the critical time, while street-lights vied with the dusk... Paul rose to his feet, took a last careful look, hurried to the bathroom, urinated into the discolored old toilet. The bathroom would smell badly for a few weeks. But no one would be troubled.

He wasted no time returning to the window. Destiny might have selected this exact ironic opportunity to bring Si sauntering along the street, a perfect target, but too quick for Paul to take aim.

Van Buren Avenue remained empty. No Si. Dusk waned; the street-lights threw a more confident glare. In the Bethea living room a light went on. Paul saw Vinnie come in, move here and there. He watched without interest. Even if Si appeared, he would hardly dare to fire through the window. The path of the bullet could be traced; the trail would lead directly from bullet-path to McAteel Realty to Jeff Pettigrew to himself.

Gally came home. Her shoulders sagged; she looked wan and dispirited. Paul felt a pang. Poor little Gally, sweet little Gally... She went into the house, he saw her in the front room. She spoke to someone out of Paul's range of vision. Si? Vinnie? Ainsworth? There was no way of knowing.

There were sounds behind Paul: creaks, sighs, rustling. The house was dark and losing its heat.

Paul looked uncomfortably over his shoulder. Too bad he'd come without a thermos of coffee. He looked at his watch, but the hands blurred in the sallow glow of the street-light. Nine o'clock? Hardly much later. If Si were in the house he'd undoubtedly be emerging shortly. If he were carousing at Samphire's, no telling when he'd be home.

Patience. Paul's eyelids drooped. He rose to his feet, walked back and forth beside the window. Tiring of the exercise he resumed his seat.

Time passed. Another hour? Paul yawned. The room was chilly. Reality had become the world as seen through the window; behind was shadow, primitive chaos. The house creaked. Rats? Sagging timbers? Paul heard a soft sound, a scrape. He turned his head, listened. Then he rose to his feet, walked quietly to the door. There was nothing to be heard. Queer. Uncertainly Paul resumed his vigil at the window. Van Buren Avenue had become infinitely drab, uninteresting. Paul felt a surfeit of the whole business. He'd leave tomorrow for Mexico City, if he could afford it... But money was lacking, money was the reason he sat here in the darkness. Very well, thought Paul, that would be his goal: five thousand dollars, then departure for the far places. He might even take Gally... Impracticable, of course. In fact, impossible...

Another sound: a thump, a scrape. No mistake this time. Paul grasped the flashlight, sprang to his feet. The sound had come from the lower floor, at the foot of the stairs. With the rifle in his right hand, the flashlight in his left, he walked to the door.

The darkness was absolute. But now there was a variation to the odor, a pungent harshness he could not immediately identify. And there was a pressure in the air, an urgency.

From the foot of the stairs came a thud, a rustling... Paul leveled the gun, switched on the flashlight. The beam of light fell along old treads, the worn linoleum of the empty hall; met an empty cardboard box at the foot of the stairs. The box was tied to a string which led up the stairs. Paul stared at the string. Why string? A pull from the second floor meant a thump and scrape from the first. Paul whirled in his tracks. The beam of the flashlight swung around. Too late. A dark shape rushed forward, knocked rifle and flashlight out of his hands. They clattered off in the darkness. The strange odor identified itself: stale cigar smoke. Hands clutched his side, his neck. Paul made a bleating noise. He kicked, grappled, elbowed; he and his opponent both fell, rolled down the steps. Paul came to a stop first, crawled clear as his adversary struck the spot where he had landed. He groped for something to strike with; his hands met an article, he grasped it and swung: the cardboard box. It hit with a resonant drum-like sound, Paul ran to the wall. For a moment there was only the sound of breathing in the hall. Paul moved cautiously toward the door. He stopped short. His enemy was near at hand. Paul's knees felt weak and loose.

A voice said, "White boy, now I'm gonna pay you back. You ran me down, now you know what I'm gonna do? I'm gonna cut you."

Paul rushed for the door. A shape dark and immensely heavy collided with him, fingers jerked at his hair. Paul tried to yell, but produced only a thin wailing sound.

"Lissen to de rooster crow," said the voice.

Paul struck, kicked; the hand in his hair yanked with enormous strength: he felt a burning looseness at his throat, a gush of warmth. His voice became a hiss from under his chin. He slumped, sat, leaned forward, clutching at his throat. He felt no pain, but he knew he was dying. Like passing out drunk, thought Paul with surprise. There was too much excitement for fear. His thoughts became silent. For a period he saw a swirling of bright colors, patterns in blue and green and red. These continued several minutes, though his body was useless.

The colors seethed and swirled, gradually paled and became transparent, as the brain cells died from want of oxygen.

Si shook his head sadly. "Like I say, I just figger to give that man a good beatin'. I go to that house, I open up the door, I go in. But he sees me comin', he jumps me, he hit me on the head. I go down. He say, 'Now you black son-of-a-bitch, I gonna shoot you.' He aims that gun, but I grab his legs. Just by luck I grab out my pocket-knife, and too bad but he get cut. I sure don't mean to hurt him." Si shook his head dolefully. "I sure don't figger things the way they turn out. When I see what's happened, I get out fast. That's all I got to tell you."

Chapter XVI

The Creed

Neil Hubbard, responding to Shaw's telephone message, appeared at the City Hall and was conducted into Shaw's office. He looked anxious, careworn; the flesh hung loose beside his mouth; the hair lay on his scalp like a blanched cabbage leaf.

"Sit down," said Shaw.

Hubbard blinked at the crispness of Shaw's voice, but without comment seated himself.

Shaw held out his hand. "Let's have it."

Hubbard passed over the black loose-leaf notebook.

Shaw placed the notebook in the exact center of his desk. He spoke in a measured voice. "I suppose you realize that the police don't sympathize with conduct like yours."

Hubbard made a feeble gesture. "There's a special situation here, special problems —"

"The suppression of evidence is a criminal act. You may very well go to jail, if the District Attorney decides to prosecute."

"I felt I was acting in the best interests of the department —"

"The Police Department?"

"The Welfare Department. Perhaps I'm wrong; if so I sincerely apologize."

Shaw snorted; Hubbard held out his hands. "Try to understand my viewpoint, try to see the position I've been in!"

"It's no different from anyone else's position."

Hubbard shook his head energetically. "I learn that one of my men is a racketeer, betraying his clients, betraying the department. Then, he's murdered — and Mr. Big is dead. If the killing can be cleared up without demoralizing the department and wrecking our public relations program, where's the harm?"

"I don't plan to argue either law or ethics with you," said Shaw. "You impeded our investigations, and we don't appreciate it."

"As I say, my motives were only to protect the department to the best of my ability."

Shaw asked quietly, "How did you find Paul Gunther's residence."

"It was Tuesday evening, after talking to you. I found two letters on Gunther's desk. One was his bank statement, with a number of cancelled checks. I examined all these carefully and found a check marked: April Rent for House at 2050½ Corinth Street."

"So?"

Hubbard leaned back in his chair. "I visited this address. No one was at home. There was no lock on the door and I went in. I found Gunther's briefcase — and that notebook. When I saw the chart, listing the names and the schedule of payments, the whole sordid affair was clear to me. Next day I learned Gunther had been killed. I sent out letters to those people Gunther had been victimizing, instructing them to send no more money to 'Mr. Big'." Hubbard shook his head furiously. "When I think of how the newspapers would have twisted this, I have no qualms whatever in suppressing that notebook. Especially in view of the 'Creed'." Hubbard spoke the word with enormous distaste. "Have you seen the 'Creed'?"

"I haven't seen anything yet." Shaw opened the notebook. Hubbard leaned forward, looked over Shaw's arm. On the first page of the notebook Paul had pasted a pencil sketch of himself, done by a skillful if sentimental hand. His eyes looked candidly from the page; his mouth had been strengthened, the capricious quirk ignored. *Paul, with all my love, Sandra,* read the dedication.

"How he saw himself, I suppose," said Hubbard.

The next page had been torn out: the index page, evidently that which Si Bethea had appropriated. Each of the next fifty-five pages was devoted to one of Paul's clients, listing name, address, particulars of their offenses against the Welfare Department, money received and the corresponding date.

"Very neat and methodical," said Shaw.

Hubbard's voice quivered. "It's the most cynical betrayal I've ever heard of!"

Shaw turned several pages and came to a list of titles, with the authors' names appended.

"Books I've never heard of," declared Hubbard aggrievedly. "*The Unquiet Grave,* by Cyril Connolly; *Poems,* James Oppenheim. Baudelaire, of course I know, and Ezra Pound... Colin Wilson... Who is Ernest Trope? James Dunne? Never heard of them... *A Theory of Personality,* Warden Hulme... *Nexus. Sexus. Plexus*... What in God's name is that? All odd-ball stuff..."

Shaw turned the page.

"Quotations," Hubbard remarked. "Apparently ideas which appealed to him."

"He has a meticulous mind," said Shaw. He turned pages and came upon a list of girls' names, each followed by a coded reference.

"Meticulous is right," sniffed Hubbard. "I can imagine what this represents."

Shaw turned another page, and came to a bold heading: *CREED,* with the subheading *Testament of Faith.*

"There it is," said Hubbard. "Read it."

Shaw read:

> I am Garnett Paul Gunther. I am alone in the universe; this is the extent of my perceptions; this is primitive reality.
>
> I am Individuality, an intensity which requires an entire universe for containment.
>
> I am unique. The universe which surrounds me is mine, but outside my control. I control I. Destiny controls the universe.
>
> Speculation: Am I more intense than Destiny?
> Am I feared? I am allowed only a single dimension in time, curtailed perceptions.
> Am I the same threat to Destiny that Destiny is to me?

Speculation: I am dynamic, masculine:
This is the I principle. Destiny, crafty, diffuse, captious, is sexless. Is there a female principle, she and I forming a duality? If so, I will necessarily encounter her. I will be alert. What a miracle when we meet!
Splendor, gold, jewels: what are they?

I am I, among shadow-shapes, not truly real.
I can do as I will with this world. If I act boldly, I overcome Destiny. If I retreat, I succumb.
Hence: I will be courageous, swift, relentless.

If this sequence of thought is a trick of Destiny to plunge me into ludicrous tragedy, I can not know. I think not. I am I, unique.
I shall not shrink back from direct deeds.
I shall fear nothing; nothing can affect me, nothing can influence me.
I can only die once.

Article 1: Destiny confronts me with various situations, personalities, perceptions. In spite of apparent diversity, a pattern must exist.
Problem: Learn this pattern.

Article 2: The numberless faces and personalities have no real existence except as they are elements in the universe. The attitudes, emotions, appetites, protests of these presences are unreal, of no more weight to me than an oil-film to the ocean.
Corollary: My own person, as distinct from my brain, is no less real or unreal than the shadow-shapes. Physical pain is an illusion.
Task: overcome pain. With concentration pain becomes a dull sensation.

Article 3: Virtues are rules in the game of life, designed to impede me. I must be careful contravening them and do so only when I am in a position of vantage over Destiny.

Article 4: Trust the faith of no person, trust the stability of no fact. Behind my back, outside the range of my vision is — what? Chaos?

Article 5: To inconvenience myself for someone else's benefit is to deplete my potentiality. Destiny will tempt me to sympathy and irrational generosity. Beware.

Article 6: Destiny will confront me with various emergencies. This is the Great Game. The Active defeats the Passive. If I act I win, if I react, I lose.

Article 7: I have unalterable faith in myself, nothing else. There is no other entity or institution to inspire faith. I trust only myself; I can never doubt the range of my capabilities—for if I doubt, I compromise my dynamic assault against Destiny.

Article 8: Destiny: the Ultimate Adversary. I can win. I can defeat Destiny. How? That is my problem.

The rest of the notebook was empty. Shaw looked up, met Hubbard's pale glance.

"Goofy," said Hubbard. "Plain goofy."

Shaw read: " 'Destiny, the Ultimate Adversary. I can win, I can defeat Destiny. How? That is the problem.' " He mused, "It's a problem for all of us."

"I pray for guidance," said Hubbard. "That is my answer."

Shaw heaved a deep sigh. "You prayed for guidance when you held out this book on me?"

"I did."

"If you get sent to jail, you'd better change your religion ... That's all for now."

Hubbard rose to his feet, reached tentatively for the book. Shaw looked up and Hubbard withdrew his hand. "Well then — good afternoon," said Hubbard. He hesitated, stumbled over his words. "I'm sorry if you feel I've made difficulties, but I only —"

"Yes, Mr. Hubbard," said Shaw. "I understand. Good afternoon."

Hubbard departed.

About the Author

Jack Vance was born in 1916 to a well-off California family that, as his childhood ended, fell upon hard times. As a young man he worked at a series of unsatisfying jobs before studying mining engineering, physics, journalism and English at the University of California Berkeley. Leaving school as America was going to war, he found a place as an ordinary seaman in the merchant marine. Later he worked as a rigger, surveyor, ceramicist, and carpenter before his steady production of sf, mystery novels, and short stories established him as a full-time writer.

His output over more than sixty years was prodigious and won him three Hugo Awards, a Nebula Award, a World Fantasy Award for lifetime achievement, as well as an Edgar from the Mystery Writers of America. The Science Fiction and Fantasy Writers of America named him a grandmaster and he was inducted into the Science Fiction Hall of Fame.

His works crossed genre boundaries, from dark fantasies (including the highly influential *Dying Earth* cycle of novels) to interstellar space operas, from heroic fantasy (the *Lyonesse* trilogy) to murder mysteries featuring a sheriff (the Joe Bain novels) in a rural California county. A Vance story often centered on a competent male protagonist thrust into a dangerous, evolving situation on a planet where adventure was his daily fare, or featured a young person setting out on a perilous odyssey over difficult terrain populated by entrenched, scheming enemies.

Late in his life, a world-spanning assemblage of Vance aficionados came together to return his works to their original form, restoring material cut by editors whose chief preoccupation was the page count of a pulp magazine. The result was the complete and authoritative *Vance Integral Edition* in 44 hardcover volumes. Spatterlight Press is now publishing the VIE texts as ebooks, and as print-on-demand paperbacks.

Colophon

This book was printed using Adobe Arno Pro as the primary text font, with NeutraFace used on the cover.

This title was created from the digital archive of the Vance Integral Edition, a series of 44 books produced under the aegis of the author by a worldwide group of his readers. The VIE project gratefully acknowledges the editorial guidance of Norma Vance, as well as the cooperation of the Department of Special Collections at Boston University, whose John Holbrook Vance collection has been an important source of textual evidence.

Special thanks to R.C. Lacovara, Patrick Dusoulier, Koen Vyverman, Paul Rhoads, Chuck King, Gregory Hansen, Suan Yong, and Josh Geller for their invaluable assistance preparing final versions of the source files.

Digitize: Mark Adams, Richard Chandler, Joel Hedlund, Dave Worden; Diff: Damien G. Jones, David A. Kennedy; Tech Proof: Hans van der Veeke; Text Integrity: Paul Rhoads, Norma Vance; Implement: Paul Rhoads; Security: Paul Rhoads; Compose: John A. Schwab; Comp Review: Christian J. Corley, Marcel van Genderen, Charles King, Paul Rhoads, Robin L. Rouch; Update Verify: Rob Friefeld, Charles King, Bob Luckin, Paul Rhoads, Tim Stretton; RTF-Diff: Erik Arendse, Charles King; Textport: Patrick Dusoulier, Charles King; Proofread: Neil Anderson, Michel Bazin, Mark Bradford, Martin Green, Lucie Jones, David A. Kennedy, A.G. Kimlin, Lee Lewis, Robert Melson, Eric Newsom, Simon Read, Paul Rhoads, Hans van der Veeke

Artwork (maps based on original drawings by Jack and Norma Vance):

Paul Rhoads, Christopher Wood

Book Composition and Typesetting: Joel Anderson

Art Direction and Cover Design: Howard Kistler

Proofing: Patrick Dusoulier, Steve Sherman, Dave Worden

Jacket Blurb: John Vance

Management: John Vance, Koen Vyverman